BLU

Praise f

It was only a matter of time before a clever publisher realized that there is an audience for whom *Exile on Main Street* or *Electric Ladyland* are as significant and worthy of study as *The Catcher in the Rye* or *Middlemarch* … The series … is freewheeling and eclectic, ranging from minute rock-geek analysis to idiosyncratic personal celebration
—*The New York Times Book Review*

Ideal for the rock geek who thinks liner notes just aren't enough
—*Rolling Stone*

One of the coolest publishing imprints on the planet—*Bookslut*

These are for the insane collectors out there who appreciate fantastic design, well-executed thinking, and things that make your house look cool. Each volume in this series takes a seminal album and breaks it down in startling minutiae. We love these. We are huge nerds—*Vice*

A brilliant series … each one a work of real love—*NME* (UK)

Passionate, obsessive, and smart—*Nylon*

Religious tracts for the rock 'n' roll faithful—*Boldtype*

[A] consistently excellent series—*Uncut* (UK)

We … aren't naive enough to think that we're your only source for reading about music (but if we had our way … watch out). For those of you who really like to know everything there is to know about an album, you'd do well to check out Bloomsbury's "33⅓" series of books—*Pitchfork*

For reviews of individual titles in the series, please visit our blog at 333sound.com and our website at http://www.bloomsbury. com/musicandsoundstudies Follow us on Twitter: @333books Like us on Facebook: https://www.facebook.com/33.3books

For a complete list of books in this series, see the back of this book.

Forthcoming in the series:

Diamond Dogs by Glenn Hendler
The Wild Tchoupitoulas by Bryan Wagner
Timeless by Martin Deykers
Tin Drum by Agata Pyzik
Voodoo by Faith A. Pennick
xx by Jane Morgan
Band of Gypsys by Michael E. Veal
Judy at Carnegie Hall by Manuel Betancourt
From Elvis in Memphis by Eric Wolfson
Ghetto: Misfortune's Wealth by Zach Schonfeld
I'm Your Fan: The Songs of Leonard Cohen by Ray Padgett
Suicide by Andi Coulter
The Velvet Rope by Ayanna Dozier
Blue Moves by Matthew Restall
Live at the Harlem Square Club, 1963 by Colin Fleming
Murder Ballads by Santi Elijah Holley
Once Upon a Time by Alex Jeffery
Tapestry by Loren Glass
The Archandroid by Alyssa Favreau
Avalon by Simon Morrison
Rio by Annie Zaleski
Vs. by Clint Brownlee

and many more …

Blue Lines

Ian Bourland

BLOOMSBURY ACADEMIC
NEW YORK · LONDON · OXFORD · NEW DELHI · SYDNEY

BLOOMSBURY ACADEMIC
Bloomsbury Publishing Inc
1385 Broadway, New York, NY 10018, USA

BLOOMSBURY, BLOOMSBURY ACADEMIC and the Diana logo are
trademarks of Bloomsbury Publishing Plc

First published in the United States of America 2020

Copyright © Ian Bourland, 2020

Cover design: 333sound.com

Library of Congress Cataloging-in-Publication Data
Names: Stockton, Will. | Gilson, D. (Duane)
Title: 33⅓ B-sides / edited by Will Stockton and D. Gilson.
Description: New York, NY : Bloomsbury Academic, 2019. | Includes
bibliographical references and index.
Identifiers: LCCN 2019008330 (print) | LCCN 2019009950 (ebook) | ISBN
9781501342424 (ePDF) | ISBN 9781501342448 (ePub) | ISBN 9781501342455
(pbk. : alk. paper) | ISBN 9781501342943 (hardback : alk. paper)
Subjects: LCSH: Popular music–History and criticism.
Classification: LCC ML3470 (ebook) | LCC ML3470 .A16 2019 (print) |
DDC 781.6409–dc23
LC record available at https://lccn.loc.gov/2019008330

ISBN: PB: 978-1-5013-3969-1
ePDF: 978-1-5013-3971-4
eBook: 978-1-5013-3970-7

Series: 33⅓

Typeset by Deanta Global Publishing Services, Chennai, India
Printed and bound in the United States of America

To find out more about our authors and books visit www.bloomsbury.com
and sign up for our newsletters.

Contents

Track Listing   vi

Introduction   1
1   Cider Punks   9
2   Five Man Army   21
3   The Coach House   37
4   The Tricky Kid   53
Interlude: Living in My Headphones   67
5   The Cherry Bear Organization   81
6   Flammable Materials   97
7   Daydreaming   109
8   Big Wheel Keeps on Turning   125

Notes   135

Track Listing

1. "Safe from Harm" (5:18)
2. "One Love" (4:48)
3. "Blue Lines" (4:21)
4. "Be Thankful for What You've Got" (4:09)
5. "Five Man Army" (6:04)
6. "Unfinished Sympathy" (5:08)
7. "Daydreaming" (4:14)
8. "Lately" (4:26)
9. "Hymn of the Big Wheel" (6:36)

Introduction

Massive Attack's first full-length record *Blue Lines* was a warning shot in the new British Invasion of the 1990s, and a harbinger of what it might have been. If you remember the era as a time of Mancunian sneers, tabloid fisticuffs, and epic guitar rock, Massive was a marked counterpoint. They replaced nostalgia with futurity, a whitey rock 'n' roll format with a notably afro-diasporic one. They showed that England was more than lads and pints, as a cosmopolitan hub that would define European life—and dance music—for most of the 1990s and beyond. A knowing alchemy of soul hooks, hip-hop production, dub instrumentation, and urbane lyrical stanzas, *Blue Lines* was an opening salvo of an age to come, one that was more world-weary, more optimistic, and more interconnected all at once. The year was 1991, the long 1980s of Margaret Thatcher and Ronald Reagan was over, and the people marginalized by conservativism and its visions of cultural purity had reason for optimism. An era of musical sophistication, sensual contemplation, and new freedoms seemed to beckon, the yobs and Little Englanders be damned.

Some may say they've never heard of Massive Attack, but the sonic palette they ushered in provided the mise-en-scène for a great deal of popular culture. This was especially true in an increasingly integrated Europe, but also in global cities where new forms of electronic music cross-pollinated through raves and megaclubs, downtown bars and after-hours cafés—from Washington, DC, to Mexico, DF, from Tel Aviv to Tokyo. There was a new, borderless map of pop music just starting to unfold, and records like *Blue Lines*, with all of its stylistic catholicism, were its lingua franca.

Blue Lines conjures a specific time and place, but also envisions a dreamy placelessness, which is why it has often been called introspective or minimal. There's an intimacy and interiority to it that plays well basically anywhere with buildings and nighttime. If you missed that, you probably saw the movie *Hackers* in 1995, heard the song "Protection," with its spare wah-wah guitar and subtle breakbeat drifting under Tracey Thorn's heartswelling lyrics. It's the soundscape for the arch gen-X romance between Angelina Jolie and Jonny Lee Miller—unsentimental, but somehow sincere. "Protection" remains insistently familiar and, although it appeared on the 1994 follow-up to *Blue Lines*, its production and its sonic textures are emblematic of a style and ethos that the record conceived. The song defines a cinematic and urban sensibility that was very much of its time and, indeed, many people's deep memory pathways. With the exception of "Motown Philly" or "Smells Like Teen Spirit," it is the defining song of the early 1990s. Or, at least, the aural embodiment of a world coming into focus that was often defiantly and self-consciously "global."

Of course, much of the optimism of the 1990s and its so-called "New World Order" feel misplaced in hindsight. Back then, the Cold War was over, prosperity and multiculturalism seemed to be on the march. But with Brexit and the Grenfell Tower inferno and the ascent of the far-right, it feels like the bad-old-days of the 1980s again—or worse. It's bittersweet to look back on the comparative exuberance and innocence of that time. And Massive's own material grew darker, more serious as the years wore on.

I'm not arguing here that *Blue Lines* was the group's best record—that would be 1998's *Mezzanine*, a definitive masterpiece with a coherent sound (all minor keys and subtle instrumentation). But *Mezzanine* is heavy listening. It's suffused by a shadowy monochrome that looks ahead into the next decade, one defined by a global war on terror, surveillance, and all the rest. Its opener, "Angel," was used to great effect in *The West Wing*, the unnerving crescendo as the President's daughter is abducted by foreign agents. It also frames an inferno at a trailer park as Brad Pitt looks on, enraged, in *Snatch* (2000). And, of course, "Tear Drop" featured as the intro to dark medical drama *House,* which closed out the aughts on an acidic note.

Which is to say that *Mezzanine* revealed Massive as artists: people who make elegant, difficult work; people who name records after obscure islands in the North Sea; people who seem to disappear for years on end, sometimes resurfacing to tour with avant-garde filmmaker Adam Curtis, or speak out against a venue in Bristol named in honor of a prominent slave trader. *Mezzanine* is the kind of record that "serious" people take seriously, but it's no one's favorite record. It doesn't conjure warm memories or happy firsts.

Not so of *Blue Lines*. This is true of everyone I spoke to at a wedding in London last year, most of whom lit up with recognition when I told them about this project. If you are between the ages of thirty and fifty (as they were), there's a good chance that some part of *Blue Lines* factored into a perfect evening, or some romantic interlude during a formative time in your life. For me, it was moving to the American East Coast, experiencing lonely, hibernal walks for the first time, experiencing the big city, Europe, and many other things for the first time too, usually with *Blue Lines* on my Discman, murmuring along with Robert Del Naja and "living in my headphones . . . ." The hip-hop journalist Michael Gonzalez recalls *Blue Lines* as the soundtrack to a voyage to Paris in 1997, driving into the countryside near Versailles with a lady, "Be Thankful for What You Got" pulsing away on the speakers. For music-video director Baillie Walsh, enlisted by Massive to visualize what was, to most, an anonymous studio project, the record was a revelation, a series of textured vignettes that inspired short films in his mind.

So while *Mezzanine* is the album built to stand the test of time, *Blue Lines*, as meandering and precocious as it is, lives on in hearts and minds of its listeners. Even so, I venture that all the recognizable facets of the Massive Attack they would become are there, on *Blue Lines*: the wide-ranging palette of influences; a rootedness in diasporic textures and production styles; a merger of the atmospheric, introspective, and cerebral; and, crucially, a subtle but distinct political edge.

Critics were kind then, and history has been especially kind in retrospect. But *Blue Lines* was not a masterwork that arrived, as it may have seemed, from left field, fully formed. Massive were emissaries of several larger scenes, and they found themselves at the right place at the right time. Importantly, they came of age and aligned themselves with the rich and diverse musical underground of Bristol in the 1980s, a proving ground and wellspring that came to fruition as the Wild Bunch sound system became Massive, and collaborators such as Nellee Hooper went on to work with the likes of Sinead O'Connor.

And on the topic of Bristol, I should note that this book places no stock in the idea of the "Bristol sound" that so fascinated music journalists looking for a hook or a marketing angle in the years after *Blue Lines* was released. After all, Grantley "Daddy G" Marshall himself wanted listeners to look beyond that connection because, "it gives the wrong impression. Because people will expect it to sound like something—the Bristol sound—which it ain't."[1]

A few caveats here. For one, this book is not a fanboy letter or a critical hagiography. I'm a historian, so I tend to think about artifacts like *Blue Lines* as enmeshed in the culture and politics of where they were produced. This doesn't mean that *Blue Lines* was a kind of passive transcription of the times— far from it. It and records like it were effectively histories of people written out of the history books, and it arguably set the tone of what the world to come could and should look like. But I'm also not necessarily suggesting that Massive were rogue geniuses, that *Blue Lines* is the greatest record of blah, blah, blah. As Marshall later recounted, "We were lazy

Bristol twats . . . It was Neneh [Cherry] who kicked our asses and got us in the studio. We recorded a lot at her house, in her baby's room. What we were trying to do was create dance music for the head rather than the feet."[2]

Then again, Robert Del Naja, Grantley Marshall, and Andrew Vowles knew what played in the underground—they were good selectors, had good taste, knew which sounds might gel into something new. More importantly, they knew how to attract the right collaborators—people like Cherry, Walsh, Cameron McVey, Jonny Dollar, Smith & Mighty, Shara Nelson, Horace Andy, and others who could see the songs in what were, at the time, often inchoate ideas. They knew to strike when the iron was hot, signing a major-label deal with Virgin where others did not. And they were served well by a sense of openness and curiosity, a willingness to see where paths led rather than follow the well-charted course of the industry and their big-time peers.

A final note: this is compiled from my own archival research and interviews. Massive themselves are aware of this book but repeatedly declined to be interviewed. This is unsurprising: much like another rainy city that burst onto the global stage in 1991—Seattle—Bristol and its musicians seem to still suffer a long hangover and a good degree of weariness about the period. Like their Seattle counterparts, fame and celebrity were not the coin of the realm. Perversely, in the wake of *Blue Lines*, Bristol became a site of media frenzy, with journalists from around the world dropping in to get a story, and lookie-loos adding a new "x" on their map of vicarious cultural tourism. Beyond that, the current personnel of the group take the line of many artists—on the street and in the gallery—of letting the work speak for itself.

With that in mind, I owe a thank-you to all the folks who did care to talk and share their stories. This is a book about a record, but also about the lives and labor of dozens of people. At the time of its creation, *Blue Lines* was an experiment, a missive from the outside. In the end, it kicked the doors of the mainstream open to the margins, in the process shifting the course of popular music.

1
Cider Punks

Anyone involved in the Bristol music scene of the 1980s will invariably bring the conversation back around to a multistory bar at 52 Park Row called the Dugout. With its dingy carpet, orange walls, and precipitous staircase, it was located in the rough geographic center of the city. Now a Chinese restaurant, the former club was a stone's throw from the university, and served as a crossroads during a time in which subculture had higher stakes—when rivalries among factions meant a Saturday on the town often led to harsh words, or worse. The Bristol of the years 1979–82 was divided by neighborhoods, to be sure, but also by affiliation and affinity. There were punks, skins, soul boys, Rastas, and Blitz-styled New Romantics. There were new-wavers, football supporters, and, as Robert del Naja tells it, parachute-pant-wearing kung fu film fanatics carrying nunchaku. "Bristol was tough on a Saturday night. If you looked alternative you would get your head kicked in! In those days you wore everything on your sleeve—walking home from school with dyed hair and a skinny tie was running the gauntlet."[1]

But the Dugout was where all walks came together, a node where people exchanged ideas, traded cassettes, and watched music videos in a lounge in the back. In the wake of the punk explosion of 1976, places like the Dugout were where the jittery sounds that became synonymous with "post punk" actively cross-pollinated and mutated, where funk horns met the druggy reverb of dub, and where hip-hop breakbeats and b-boy culture would find a beachhead amid young audiences still suffering the long hangover of cock rock and the excesses of prog. Anything without a guitar appealed, and the DIY ethos of punk complemented the cut-and-paste sonic appropriations of turntablism and MCing. In those years before the advent of the producer-as-celebrity or "curated playlists," the DJ played a crucial role. They were the person behind the record players who laid down the beat, a substrate for new lyrical flows over familiar material. And in places like Bristol, the DJ found their equivalent at a different sort of party—the "selector" who charted the course of the evening at dub sound systems.

The Dugout, open seven nights a week, had their own forward-looking DJ in the person of Grantley Marshall. He was not yet part of the celebrated local Wild Bunch sound system but already developing the blend of styles that would characterize the sessions for which the group would come to be known as they organized their underground parties throughout the mid-1980s. The Wild Bunch, a loose collective forged in the spirit of those early, inchoate years of hip-hop would, of course, spawn the side project Massive Attack by decade's end. And Marshall, along with Del Naja, is a constant that connects the old days at the Dugout to the auteurish version of Massive that persists to this day. While his tastes were wide ranging, it's long been said that Marshall brought the hip-hop/reggae side of things to the studio, a complement to Del Naja's punk enthusiasms.

For all that, it's tough to overstate the degree to which punk, as an ethos, was a catalyzing force in the Bristol landscape. There were no more hard-and-fast rules; you could do it yourself, even if you weren't classically trained or well connected. The ur-moment in this worldview was the June 4, 1976, gig that the Sex Pistols played at the Lesser Free Hall in Manchester, attended by a mix of working-class locals and soon-to-be post-punk icons, from the Buzzcocks founders Pete Shelley and Howard Devoto to the Smiths' lachrymose frontman Morrissey. It was the first of two shows they would play there during that high summer of punk rock, and indeed, the second, better-attended show helped galvanize Factory Records, Joy Division, and an entire history ranging from goth rock to the Madchester rave scene.

The Pistols were not especially good that week—just the opposite. But they showed that an entire generation of kids suffering the privations of unemployment, fuel shortages, blackouts, and the grim prospect of life in England during the 1970s could find creative redemption by building new subcultural worlds. There was the dandyish pomp of clubs like the Blitz in London and the overlapping rosters of reggae, northern soul, queer disco, and youthful punks at pubs and performance halls. They worked collectively in the working-class districts of Hammersmith or St. Pauls, British youth creating their own hidden utopias, their own forms of public address. From safety pins and badges to dyed hair, rococo jackets, and sharp rude-boy tailoring, they alienated their elders and forged new sites of conflict and collaboration. In short, that Sex Pistols gig gave the postwar generation something to live for, and a sense that they could write their own rules. According to the journalist David Nolan, in the summer of 1976, "the audience who were in there that night . . . turned to each other and said, in that Mancunian way: "'That's rubbish! We could do so much better than that.' And that's exactly what they did."[2]

These worlds all converged in Bristol at the Dugout. Rob Smith, later to become one half of the local duo Smith & Mighty, had come from a working-class area to the north, and recalls alighting on the center city during a time when no one seemed to be working. Everyone was halfheartedly trying to learn an instrument, and the Dugout was at the heart of it all:

> People complained about it all the time, "Oh, bloody hell we're going to the Dugout again." But the truth is, there were so many tribes in Bristol at the time, because there was a lot of scenes going on, there was like the soul boys and the jazz guys and jazz funk guys and the mirror posse—the guys who used to dance in front of the mirror and all that. And then there's the dreads and punks and goths, rockabillies, and everybody's thing is in this club. And so, you have this real blending of people.[3]

The Dugout became a natural hub for the city's diverse subcultures. But the denizens of early 1980s Bristol had another advantage: time. The welfare state had not yet been hollowed out, and the widespread unemployment that Smith recalls was counterbalanced by initiatives by national grants and local councils and, of course, the public assistance known as the dole. It was much like the hip-hop and punk-infused ecosystem that coalesced in Manhattan's Lower East Side during that same period. One could live cheaply and the days opened up to wide expanses of listening to records, tinkering in makeshift studios, hanging out until all hours of the night, and drifting from scene to scene on foot.

Smith himself became instrumental in this scene. By mid-decade, he installed two recording studios in his home, which became a rallying point for kids influenced by American MCs and homegrown dub and reggae. He had gotten his start with a so-called YOP (a youth opportunity grant) to put on a reggae musical called "Freedom City," headed up by local roots musician Reynold Duncan. The grant wasn't much, but it created a pretext for Smith to learn to play guitar on the job. Similarly, the convivial quality of the Caribbean sound system complemented a hip-hop that was still both performative and social. This iteration of the genre was slowly making its way to Bristol clubs in the form of videos and records and even a tour stop by Kurtis Blow, the first MC to sign a major-label deal. Bronx hip-hop, like the strains of Caribbean music that effloresced during the late 1970s in Bristol, emphasized long-hangs, the gathering of community in parks and, later, warehouses to perform, to battle, to "sound" as a show of solidarity and defiance.

This would be the blueprint by the second half of the decade for the Wild Bunch sound system that became Massive Attack: the stylistic catholicism of the Dugout, the DIY spirit of punk, and the appropriative, interactive quality of black diasporic music. For Del Naja, this resourceful spirit was key:

> The Pistols said the subculture of punk was dead after 6 months and that it had become a uniform, but for me that uniform was important as it separated me from the parts of society that didn't really understand. Hip-hop came and merged with that and took over. The idea of the sound system was around as well—build your event, your own show—that was the same kind of attitude. None of us had money or were musicians or had any instruments, so we couldn't put on concerts but we could put on sound systems and get some booze and lights and put on events in a very DIY fashion.[4]

On this side of the twenty-first century, it's easy to take for granted the way styles and sounds can crisscross the world in an instant, in an accelerated version of what happened in the 1990s, as hip-hop became an increasingly unified "lifestyle" and punk, by and large, a nostalgic simulation of its own glory days. But in the 1980s, both forms represented a broadside against authority and against institutional pieties. This, and the distance afforded by the Atlantic Ocean, meant considerable freedom to the lads in Bristol. While Massive Attack nominally continued to function as a loose collective, in the vein of the sound system party, it was (and is) anchored by a former DJ and a former punk-graffiti kid.

Before there was a Wild Bunch, Del Naja wandered among the working-class blues clubs and hole-in-wall speakeasies. Passing the time as a kind of West Country version of the Bowery Bum or Jean-Michel Basquiat squatting in Tompkins

Square Park, Del Naja and his friends would head to a local barn to top off gallon jugs with Old Cripple Crock Cider. Like gutter punks the world over, they sat in parks like Castle Green—not far from the Temple Mead's train station—deranging themselves on rough scrumpy and planning missions. These are familiar origin stories, albeit sketched in the very British tones of a coastal town and the verdant hills and plentiful orchards of Somerset and the Cotswolds.

For Smith, the strength of the Bristol scene of the 1980s was a relative sense of isolation. London was several hours away by train but worlds away psychically and dispositionally. Bristol moved at a stately pace by most accounts, which allowed for a sense of openness to where an afternoon or recording session might lead. This sense compounded on itself: he notes that "Nobody was bothered in Bristol. There was no attention from London. There was nobody coming down saying, 'Oh, you should do this, you should do that.' It was left alone to stew in its own juice for years and years." But for all that, Bristol was still a fundamentally a kind of subcultural crossroads.

Settled astride the Avon River on its course to the Bristol Channel, the city has the feel of a port city, an Atlantic entrepôt, its vast network of records shops was said to be first to get their hands on foreign imports during the 1970s and 1980s. Similarly, as a university town, Bristol sees a constant influx of young people from throughout the UK, which consistently generates fresh ranks of both audiences and instrumentalists. Indeed, the University of Bristol has long placed among the best music programs in the country, and specializes in classical and avant-garde composition and even more arcane medieval forms. The DIY zeal of the punk scene was therefore counterbalanced by virtuosic players and traditional jazz hangs. Even now, a quick walk around Bristol—from the hipper precincts of Stokes Croft to the old harbor at Spike Island—reveals a high concentration of stores selling instruments and production equipment new and used. Pubs, small clubs, and large venues dot the landscape: the grand old Colston Hall or the legendary dance club Lakota. As quiet and measured as the city is, it also has the feel of circulation, of a constant churn of people coming and going.

Part of that circulation and churn, of course, is Bristol's place on the concert tour circuit, which brings musicians from all levels of the industry to the scene. One such group was The Slits, a women-centric band who toured in 1977 with the Clash. They were virtually synonymous with UK punk, up through their major label debut, 1979's *Cut*. The Slits's touring sound op was a young reggae producer named Adrian Sherwood, who would go on to become a legendary industrial producer (KMFDM, Nine Inch Nails). And the group was brought to Bristol by a singer named Mark Stewart, who had formed his own band in 1977 with Bruce Smith (not to be confused with Rob, of Smith & Mighty), a drummer who would occasionally sit in at gigs with the Slits. Smith was also married to Neneh Cherry for a time, who in turn featured on the band's follow-up record, 1981's *Return of the Giant Slits*. For her part, Cherry—raised in Sweden and New York by stepfather Don Cherry, the avant-garde jazz trumpeter—was already immersed in the UK post-punk scene by age 17.

By then, Mark Stewart and Bruce Smith's band, The Pop Group, was an integral part of what would become known as the "Bristol sound" before that term came to mean trip-hop. That early-1980s sound fused angular reggae guitars, spacey reverb, and funk bass with the complex percussive polyrhythm and chromatic dexterity more associated with free jazz. Stewart's vocal delivery—by turns yipping and operatic—and politicized lyrical content managed to foreground the emerging New Wave sound. It also echoed the American hardcore scene coming into focus back across the Atlantic. Their 1980 outing for Rough Trade Records featured songs such as "Forces of Oppression" and "Feed the Hungry," and occupied the same discursive terrain as, for instance, the Dead Kennedys or Minor Threat.

But sonically, The Pop Group's palette was a rawer, more discordant version of a sound that would be popularized within several years (albeit in a sanded-down, radio-friendly form) by the likes of the Fixx, Gang of Four, and mid-career Talking Heads. Which is to say, The Pop Group generated, seemingly ex nihilo, the sound that acts like Franz Ferdinand are still trying to perfect. Aside from being an early favorite of Robert Del Naja, they were the stellar mass around which a host of other Bristol groups emerged during those pivotal years. One was the drum-heavy Mouth, founded by Rob Merrill, Andy Guy, Nellee Hooper, and Jamie Hill and based out of the Hill's apartment in the Clifton neighborhood.[5] Mouth toured with the Slits and the celebrated roots-reggae band Talisman.

Another group, Rip Rig + Panic, was named for a record by the midwestern free-jazz titan Rahsaan Roland Kirk and formed in 1980 as a telescoping lineup of former Pop Group members (Gareth Sager, Bruce Smith), featuring Cherry on vocals. Cherry recalls falling into the Bristol scene as a "dazed and confused" teenager, still rebelling, but soon connecting with RR + P, "people who were into the music I'd grown up with" but also able to channel a spirit of simultaneous chaos and innocence: the "whole punk thing was very important."[6]

If this is all starting to read like a tangled web, it is—and that's the point. At the dawn of the 1980s, Bristol, a town of under 500,000 people, had become a vital hub. It was not only home to a range of cosmopolitan sounds from the underground, but served as a petri dish where they could hybridize and multiply. These new sonic pathways were synonymous with what we call post-punk, and, more distinctly, they fused together diasporic musics such as jazz, reggae, funk, and (certainly by 1983) the two-turntable model and lyrical meter of American hip-hop. The Dugout, with "Daddy G" Marshall at the helm, would be one site of this admixture, as were the free-wheeling Wild Bunch sound system parties that took up the mantle of the Dugout upon its close in 1986.

While they were primarily a vehicle for live performance, the Wild Bunch did record for a time. Their first major release, 1988's *Friends & Countrymen* starts as garden variety fare of the sort one might have heard back in New York, but gives over to something else altogether—"The Look of Love," with its loping, chiming beat, orchestral scratches, and a haunting female vocal line. The song was by then a soul standard, written by the prolific pop-orchestral composer Burt Bacharach in 1967 and popularized by Dusty Springfield for the *Casino Royale* soundtrack. True to form, the record-scratched horns of the Wild Bunch version call back subtly to the modish, Ian Fleming-infused verve of the original, and presage the Portishead template with funky aplomb.[7]

As sui generis as it was, *Friends & Countrymen* was released even as key members shifted their attention to other projects. Ironically, it in some ways marked the disbanding of the group as a sound system. Yet, that final section of the record also looked ahead to the tonal quality of *Blue Lines* and the stylistic hallmarks of Smith & Mighty studios. It was during this time that Massive Attack was born, the name itself a lyrical fragment from the 1988 sessions.

It was Rob Smith who recorded Massive's debut single, "Any Love," that same year. MASS 001, as it was printed, was even funkier than its predecessor, featuring an acidy synth, snippets of sampled saxophone, and the lyrical croon of singer Carlton (who would go on to record a solo project with Smith & Mighty). When played side by side with another record from 1988—Jackie Jackson singing another Burt Bacharach tune, "Anyone Had a Heart" for Smith & Mighty's rework "Anyone"—the symmetries abound. Together, they heralded a new kind of "Bristol sound," one rooted in the experimentation The Pop Group and their orbit, but routed through an array of new (and ultimately genre-defining) digital equipment.

Others would come through the Smith & Mighty studio, including a very young Jody Wisternoff (then in hip-hop mode, but soon to be one of the mega producers Way Out West), Krissy Kris, Lynx, Kelz of 3PM, to name but a few. Their fellow travelers, such as the collective Reprazent, led by Roni Size, and DJs Krust and Die would, too, come to prominence in the opening years of the 1990s. This brief twenty-year period marked an explosion of distinctive and far-reaching musical forms and collaborations. Sociologist Peter Webb, himself part of Bristol's Statik Sound System, has argued that the city was a quintessential subcultural "milieu." The "combinations of reggae, hip-hop, funk, jazz, Punk, film soundtracks, and alternative rock can be said to be present in a number of cities within the UK," Webb notes, "but artists in Bristol have combined them in very particular ways."[8] This intricate genealogy is easier to take in visually, which is why, in 1999, the Japanese DJ Naoki compiled the "Bristol Family Orbit." A sinuous and overlapping array of people and collectives, the diagram is fit for *Homeland*'s Carrie Mathison. This chapter has merely scratched the surface.

In terms of *Blue Lines*, the headline is this: to Del Naja, the proto-Wild Bunch Bristol landscape was essential. "For me this was a crucial period and also for G. Music was in a transitional stage from 1978 to '82 . . . My record collection was so schizophrenic. It went from post-punk to reggae music." A few years later, Massive Attack would emerge from this vibrant scene already rife with tendencies that *Blue Lines* would further distill and then bring to a global audience. If the Massive sound—with its blend of hip-hop beats, electronic production, punk intransigence, and echoes of soul and reggae—floored many listeners on its release, it likely came as no surprise to folks back in the West of England.

2
Five Man Army

Robert Del Naja describes the slow filtration of American hip-hop to English shores as a catalyzing force, a sort of x-factor that solidified what would become the sound and lingua franca of the Wild Bunch. There was a protozoic period in the late 1970s marked by eclectic record bins and varied listening habits—reggae, punk, New Wave, Northern Soul. . . . Then somewhere around 1983–1984, hip-hop enters the mix, and things start to evolve quickly.

By 1988, the pieces of the Massive Attack collective were in place, including the laconic Andrew "Mushroom" Vowles—usually shorthanded as "the hip-hop guy" in the crew—along with Del Naja, Marshall, and a guy named Adrian Thawes. The beats were distinctive from the outset. But vocally, they followed a by-now familiar format. A rotating cast of MCs (black and white) would take the mic, improvising flows, battling other crews, penning thoughtful verses. If you've seen *8 Mile*, you get the gist. Early Massive sounds a lot like the Wild Bunch.

Then in 1991, *Blue Lines* is released, not made for the party, but for sustained listening. According to Marshall,

"There was a sense that there was something different that we were creating . . . at the time, dance music was this high-octane kind of music, of hedonism, escapism. We were making the type of music for after the club. You've come home and you're off your head and you want to relax."[1] It was a fully fledged record, a document of where Massive had been, and a prototype for where it would head next, with 1994's *Protection*, a shimmering refinement of its precursor. Together, these records were Exhibits A and B for what many in the press started to call a "Bristol mystique."

I wade more fully into the debates around hip-hop and "trip-hop" in the pages ahead, but for now, consider two ideas. First, the taxonomy of popular music was a bit less nuanced in those days—if it had a synth, it was electronic(a) or "techno"; if it had a breakbeat or featured a black producer, it was typically couched as some variant of "rap." But the cardinal strength of *Blue Lines*—then and now—is that it defied any easy categorization. It seemed to define something deeply rooted in place and time, but also to reach forward, into as-yet-unknown terrain.

And second, if *Blue Lines* does represent the iteration of a specific musical lineage, it was arguably a mutation of another type of black music: dub and roots styles, the one with its emphasis on sonic effects and instrumental remix, and the other with its lyric-driven excursions into liberation theology and urban storytelling. Indeed, to an American ear already steeped in golden-age hip-hop with its chunky beats and percussive spoken-word style, *Blue Lines* likely seemed a correspondence from another world. That world was not altogether unfamiliar, but it was spacier, hazier. It was slower, more subtle. A reggae world. And whatever else it meant in those days, the subgenres of reggae that predominated in the United Kingdom during the late 1970s and 1980s were notable for a few things: their attention to instrumentation and production, and their creation of parallel sonic universes. Reggae generated a distinct atmospheric tableaux amid the urban decay.

In an obvious sense, the Wild Bunch sound system—Del Naja, Vowles, Marshall, Miles Johnson, Nellee Hooper, et al.—was special because it capitalized on hip-hop's newness, its permeability. While hip-hop was definitely forged in the Bronx, it still flaunted its diasporic roots, and had not hardened into the reportage of urban American life for which it would be known.[2] It was more of a sensibility that was still being elaborated, which meant that it could also be adapted to a British landscape that was fertile ground for both punk and the variants of reggae that were, effectively, the American form's bass-cultural cousins. In short, transatlantic hip-hop and a multiethnic lineup helped define the Wild Bunch sound and visual palette, but made them relative outliers in the wider terrain of weekend sound system parties helmed by second-generation Brits from the Caribbean, crews who battled in a variety of ways. Score was kept in this world in a variety of ways: the scale and bass tone of the namesake mobile sound systems (curtain walls of speaker cabinets, a mess of mixing boards, turntables, and snaking audio cables); the quality of record selection and the ability to keep the party going well into the evening; the verbal dexterity of the MC (or in Jamaican terms, the deejay doing the "toasting"); or in the freshness of the records, having access to the newest plates from overseas or, better still, having a known reggae vocalist shout out your crew. Many readers will note immediate similarities here with DJ culture more generally, as it evolved in the 1990s and beyond, and to a then-nascent hip-hop culture as well.

The latter is unsurprising, given the rhizomic connections between a wide range of black diasporic musical forms. Clive Campbell (DJ Kool Herc), for instance, widely recognized as the founding father of hip-hop in New York,[3] merged verbal improvisation over instrumental rhythms—typical of sessions back in the Caribbean (and later, dancehall parties)—with the distinctive sounds of American funk and soul.[4] Similarly, the famed dub producer Lee "Scratch" Perry was a crucial influence on both British and American scenes, pioneering new recording techniques at his "Black Ark" in Jamaica during the 1970s, and popping up on a Beastie Boys record in 1998. In the meantime, he collaborated with Adrian Sherwood—formerly of the Slits' orbit, but more notably an impresario of British dub talent, and later a contributor and remixer for Depeche Mode, Skinny Puppy, and a gamut of industrial acts—and Neil "Mad Professor" Fraser, who would remix Massive's *No Protection* as a protracted, ethereal dub meditation in 1994–95.

Fraser's reworking of the tracks from the *Blue Lines* follow-up—already genetically encoded with reggae elements—neatly encapsulates the Caribbean inheritance of Massive Attack more generally. He takes familiar tracks and reimagines them, not by chopping the beat and rapping over it, but by expanding its aural and psychic space, drawing out and looping a bar here, dilating a melody or modulating it through synth there, drenching everything in reverb, overlaying a diaphanous shimmer throughout. Things are brought down to a sumptuous pace, the tonalities by turns aqueous expanses and angular punctuations of delay-staggered keys or stabs of guitar. *No Protection* is beyond headphone music: you set yourself adrift in it. *Blue Lines* arrays its other influences atop this scaffolding, rather than the other way around (that would be the work of, say, the Fugees or Busta Rhymes).

And there are other obvious connections still. By all accounts, *Blue Lines*'s ace in the studio was one Jonny Dollar, who cowrote "Unfinished Sympathy" and was part of the production team for both Massive and Neneh Cherry at the age of 25. Dollar (né Jonathan Sharp) was, apparently, already a veteran of the emerging dancehall scene, which was an important precursor to the jungle style of drum and bass, and blended electronic styles with Jamaican imports. He appears to be featured on a record from 1983 released on the Raiders imprint, the "first ever" live dancehall session in London, held in the borough of Lambeth, and featuring Dollar on a record played by the in-demand Nasty Rockers Sound System—a group that collaborated with a veritable who's-who of Jamaican music from Shabba Ranks to I-Roy.

To map the interconnections and cross-pollinations among the various reggae subgenres—between the sound systems and the producers whose records they played, whose dub plates they voiced over—is a daunting book-length task unto itself.[5] But suffice it to say this: reggae and its various accoutrements (like the "rockers" style of sharp dress to the new fascinations with cannabis and Rastafarianism) had become a globally recognizable force by the mid-1970s. And, as a home to tens of thousands of immigrants from the Commonwealth in the years after the Second World War, England had deep connections to the Caribbean through a vast informal network of recordings, correspondence, community organizations, and back-and-forth travel. As a result, while Jamaica remained the "Mecca," reggae, dancehall, dub, and ska scenes with distinct characters emerged throughout the United Kingdom. This created a constellation of informal spaces in which new subgenres might emerge. As leaders of their own sound system, and as producers of celebrated West country parties, the Wild Bunch occupied a key node in this system. This role was only further compounded by their work with Dollar on *Blue Lines* as well as their ongoing creative partnership with legendary reggae warbler Horace Andy.

In retrospect, it would have been odd for Massive to *not* have been immersed in Jamaican music. By the time the Wild Bunch was coming together around the locus of the Dugout, reggae had already been popularized and hybridized across the musical spectrum. Groups like the Police had taken the echoey guitar reverb and stuttering snare hits of dub music (to say nothing of Sting's forays into a bizarre, if signature patois) and made it radio friendly in tunes like 1979's "Walking on the Moon." Similarly, the Clash was but the most visible act in an ongoing alliance between anti-racist British punk and reggae groups in the aftermath of the 1976 riots at the Notting Hill Carnival. They collectively militated against the seam of nationalism increasingly apparent as the decade wore on. And Bristol itself, of course, was home to its own reggae scene, anchored by the celebrated Black Roots. Already an established live act, their 1983 record of the same name was socially conscious in its explorations, delving into the Rastafarian motifs one might expect for a record with "roots" in the title, but also into the problems of alienation and day-to-day violence experienced in many black British enclaves.

The history of this violence is a familiar one. In the decades after the Second World War, nearly 200,000 Jamaicans came to England, of which the island nation was still a colony until 1962. They crossed the ocean looking for work, which was plentiful in a country decimated by war. Predictably, the economic slump had much the same effect in late-1970s England as it has in Europe and the United States in recent years: a rush to blame immigrants, and a xenophobic turn against communities like the Caribbean enclave of St. Paul's in eastern Bristol. A series of anti-immigration measures in preceding years served as a backdrop to emergent racist skinhead groups and the anti-immigrant National Front political party. At the same time, so-called sus laws gave police license to detain "suspect" people, often based on racial profiling. As in Baltimore and Ferguson nearly forty years later, this noxious cocktail of overpolicing and economic exclusion would eventually boil over. Predictably, England was ablaze with rioting in its cities during the first half of the 1980s. The incident that kicked off this long season of discontent was the St. Paul riot of April 2, 1980.

Grosvenor Road is a high street in St. Paul's, lined with modest two- and three-flat buildings, storefronts, bodegas, and bars topped with apartments. Notable on this strip was the Black and White Café, a watering hole where people shot the breeze, played pinball or dominos, and dealt hash and weed. It was also something of a safe zone, a place police wouldn't tread without sufficient numbers—a bit like running across a church threshold and seeking amnesty. Ray Mighty of Smith & Mighty was a longtime reggae fan who had been politicized by the punk scene, and grew up around the corner. He was there, nay, joined in, the day of the riot, and had to lay low in west London for months afterward. He remembers:

> They were just messing with people so often and they caught it on the wrong the day. They were raiding, and we decided to throw a brick at a van and caught four officers on their own and they were attacked and it spiraled from there. For eight hours, there was no law. The police got run out—they didn't have the equipment or the training. They didn't want to arrest anyone for the next 4-5 years. It was a no-go area for a while.[6]

The riots that followed over the next five years—places like Toxteth in Liverpool, Brixton in London, and Handsworth in Birmingham—are well documented by visual artists like photographer Vanley Burke and the Black Audio Film Collective. These neighborhoods were the immediate backdrop for an efflorescence of art, literature, and music commonly known as the Black British Art Movement. This loose alliance built on the consciousness-raising work of activists like the British Black Panthers, dub poets like Linton Kwesi Johnson and Jean Binta Breeze, and the elevating force of Caribbean music.

As historian and then-visual activist Eddie Chambers points out, reggae music was an important social force those days, an alternative to a mainstream media controlled by the buttoned-up BBC. Rastas were radical voices among the often conservative and Christian immigrant communities, and their concerts and recordings—or the selection of their records at sound systems—became an underground network. According to Chambers, reggae and its spin-offs constituted an "extraordinarily complex dimension of reportage, and of black consciousness." Beyond the day-to-day of the city, Caribbean music spoke to issues affecting the global diaspora, serving as "a means by which certain people came to consciousness about Apartheid," life in Jamaica, and "common struggles, such as policy brutality toward spaces of blackness."[7]

Such spaces—little oases within a dominant culture inhospitable to black life—could be found in record stores like Dub Vendor in Clapham or Daddy Kool in SoHo. These were crucial pilgrimage sites where you could smoke a spliff while waiting to listen to records, and where the freshest imports could be found. During his year of exile following the St. Paul's uprising, Ray Mighty shopped at Daddy Kool, and on his return to Bristol, reggae became an important counterpoint to punk for him. He was part of another local sound system called Three Stripe, and played in a band with Rob Smith—a band with an often-absentee drummer.

As a workaround, Smith and Mighty purchased a drum machine, a Roland "Drumatix" 606, one of an array of new tools meant as practice equipment that, in the hands of a generation of kids became the building blocks of new sounds altogether. The Roland 303 didn't sound much like a bass, but its oscillating knobs gave birth to Acid House. The 606 and 808 generated the hard-edged mechanical drum snaps that were synonymous with the hip-hop breaks of the era, and would shift Smith and Mighty away from bands and into the studio. In short, what started as a makeshift strategy for shorthanded bands became a blueprint for a new kind of musicality and, eventually, a cultural phenomenon that changed music altogether.

As a result, during the 1990s and beyond, Smith & Mighty's records were a distinct blend of dub sounds and digital production techniques like sampling and looping. During the transition years around 1988, they too recorded a rework of the Burt Bacharach song. For this one, "Walk On," they used the same beat for both the A and the B sides of the single. Although it was distributed by the large indie clearinghouse Revolver Records, it bears the imprint of Mighty's sound system, and "Three Stripe Records." Of course, there are other important connections between Smith & Mighty and Massive Attack that we will return to, but it's worth noting that the idea of naming one's DIY label after a sound system crew was one that Massive themselves would adapt. Even early promo copies of what would be *Blue Lines*, a four-track cassette including "One Love" and "Unfinished Sympathy," were boldly marked as "A Wild Bunch Recording."

*****

1998's *Mezzanine* is a very different record than *Blue Lines*. The latter is in many ways an encomium of the various forces that shaped it: it is loose, collaborative, plainly subcultural.

But the former is arguably Massive's defining musical statement. *Mezzanine* is expertly produced and shorn down to a minimum of personnel, with Andrew Vowles on the outs and Tricky on to other things. It's the record that gave the world the iconic "Teardrop" and it looked ahead to a murkier atmospheric mode that was not "cinematic" in its throwbacks to Bacharach and the 1960s but instead generated altogether new sonic landscapes that would redefine what "cinematic" might mean. *Mezzanine* is guitar heavy and relies less on the sampling and synth technology of the decade prior and more on subtle instrumentation, down to wailing sitar and gamelan-style percussion. It was not, in other words, much of a reggae record. And yet, between the better-known singles, several delicate tracks hold the record together as a unified listening experience. These tracks are bracketed by two versions of the song "Exchange," which is essentially a psychedelic doo-wop song of lightly pulsing strings. The baseline and piano weave in and out, and the whole number is drenched in flanges and echoes, tricks that themselves subtly hearken back to trippy dub plates from another era.

"Exchange" is a bit of a coda to the paranoiac, thunderous material of *Mezzanine*'s opening run, and the lyrics suggest a kind of lullaby, gently lilting over the instrumental. But they contain a warning pregnant with metaphysical certitude, a parable for life in an urban Babylon: "You see a man's face/You don't see his heart/See a man's face/But you don't know his thoughts." The song's injunction to keep one's own counsel, to guard one's inner light is precisely the sort of fare one would expect from roots songs, with their spiritual horizon and distrust of human dualities. And the lyrics are indeed lifted from an earlier recording, "See a Man's Face" from Horace Andy's *Skylarking* album. Featuring a deejay interlude by Prince Moonie and recorded for the legendary Studio One in 1972, the original approaches the platonic ideal of reggae from the period. All the tonal and instrumental cues are solidly in place, while the lyrics embody the principals of Rasta life in the postcolony. The song cuts deep, beyond the fratboy clichés that became so closely associated with the genre's mainstream diffusion.

But the most important element of both "See a Man's Face" and its reworking as "Exchange" is the vocal delivery of Andy himself. I first heard his otherworldly lamentations on a first listen to *Mezzanine* the year after its release. Already, Andy was a reggae elder statesman. Yet he was essentially the star of the Massive Attack record, lending his voice not only to "Exchange," but to the noirish "Man Next Door." The lyrics of album opener, "Angel," are a stripped-down rendition of Andy's "You are my Angel." In each case, his delivery is singular, a contra tenor rarely matched in popular music, perhaps only comparable to Little Jimmy Scott or Nina Simone.

But this is where words begin to fail. No music criticism can aptly describe or translate the experience of listening to Horace Andy, any more than writing can convey the pathos of opera, or the wounded yearning of a country ballad. Andy defines a genre, but his timbre also defies categorization. While it's now commonplace (even reductive, perhaps) to connect the Caribbean with the historical weight of slavery— to define its religious forms by the permeable membrane between past and present, the sacred and profane that they traverse—in some instances, there's simply no other way to describe it. His voice is a missive from another world, haunted and spectral and fluid. On all three of Massive's records in the 1990s, Horace Andy was the secret weapon. It might be impossible to make a bad record when he's near the mic.

For this reason, the reggae chanteur was much in demand in Bristol during the Wild Bunch years. His imprimatur—a short hook or a shout out to your sound system—was worth its weight in reputational gold, the sort of coup that could put a crew over the top at a sound clash. Andy visited during Bristol at this time, occasionally turning up at a hang, or on someone's sofa (apparently, he enjoyed watching Rowan Atkinson's comic stylings). And he remembers falling in with Massive Attack by chance in 1990. Del Naja had heard his Studio One work and guest spots on other records, and was introduced by a mutual acquaintance (likely the photographer and filmmaker, Dick Jewell).

Andy, in turn, was central to three songs on *Blue Lines*. He is the primary vocalist on "One Love," a common enough injunction in reggae music more generally, in this case, reimagined as a romantic declaration over a few bars of carefully sampled and looped funk and jazz elector piano motifs. Like "Exchange," this is not much of a stand-alone track, but playing through side "A" it forms an ambient glue. "One Love" cements an unmistakable psychic tone that elevates *Blue Lines* beyond the hodge-podge of singles and castoffs that often characterized the hip-hop or dance album format.

Then there's "Five Man Army," a highpoint of the album and the one most evidently an inheritor of the UK reggae subgenres that prefigure it. This is true of the underlying track: all throbbing, spidery bass, reverb-soaked up-picks on the guitar, syncopated rim clicks and little riffs on something that sounds like a synthesized melodica. Tricky and Del Naja trade off playful, languorous verses, including the latter's concise "putting away childish things" moment: "When I was a child I played Subbuteo on/My table then I graduate to Studio One." From table-top sports to classic Jamaican music in two lines.

This is also Grantley Marshall's most obvious lyrical contribution to *Blue Lines*, and it comes in the form of dub-style deejaying, rapping in a bounding basso between verses. Andy is there too, down in the mix, here too a transmission from another plane, intoning bits and snatches of his own records—"Money is the Root of All Evil" from 1983's *Dance Hall Style* and the titular chorus from "Skylarking." Massive, of which Andy had become something of an honorary member by 1994, went on to repeat this trick on *Protection*. That album's "Spying Glass" is a mere update of "Live in the City," also from *Dance Hall Style*, and a cautionary tale of the powers that be trying to "know rasta business." "Spying Glass" rephrases the anxieties of being a spiritual man in a fallen country—a cornerstone of dread eschatology—but was also an important sociopolitical narrative in both Jamaica and England at the time of its release. Andy's description of the perils of living in an unfamiliar land and being harassed by authorities certainly rang true in places like the Handsworth or St. Paul's of the Thatcher era.

All of which is to say that on all three of their 1990s records, Massive were consciously making latter-day reggae albums, recording with one of the architects of the roots genre. But even without Horace Andy, reggae and its public performance of bass culture were the social and professional terroir from which Massive Attack emerged. Before Acid House and rave, there was the sound clash, and even as hip-hop was coming together in the Bronx, Bristol had roots, then dancehall.

3
The Coach House

If St. Paul's was the center of Caribbean life in Bristol, then Clifton was its direct counterpoint: the one in the east, the other on a hill in the west; one working class, the other affluent; one home to immigrants from the colonies, the other built on the spoils of tobacco and the slave trade. Walking around Clifton now is not unlike an afternoon in a wealthy area of London or any other inner-ring suburb. It is part of the city but also insulated from it, its streets lined with manicured hedgerows and well-appointed homes. Clifton exudes a sense of genteel calm, of long-established privilege. It seems far removed from underworlds evoked in the records for which the city is so well known.

Richmond Hill, then, is a typical street in Clifton, notable only for a rather utilitarian-looking extension building for the university looming on the west side of the street. Standing on its steps, the prospect is of neat row and three-flat Georgetown town homes in a sagey green. But on closer inspection, situated across a driveway and tucked in a backyard is a low-slung structure with a sloped roof and dingy French doors. It looks like the sort of place one might store a pile of old canoes, weathered boxes of papers, or a teenager exiled from the main house. It's a small building, scarcely big enough for a car or carriage but it is, nonetheless, known locally as the Coach House. During its ten-year run, it was a studio of note, boasting recordings by the Blue Aeroplanes and Neneh Cherry and, as anyone in Bristol can tell you, helped birth *Blue Lines*.

Many accounts of Massive Attack give the impression that their entire first LP was conceived and executed solely at the Coach House. In fact, only half of *Blue Lines*'s tracks list the studio. But many were recorded there, and the idiosyncratic setup the group found at Coach House served as a site of sonic experimentation and iteration, its warm acoustics and deft engineering responsible for the balance of familiar and unfamiliar on *Blue Lines*. It may have been possible to make that album anywhere, but there is an unmistakable tonal quality in its grooves, a kind of aural umami that it shares with Portishead's *Dummy* (a profoundly different project by a profoundly different group) that casual listeners likely mistake as that elusive "Bristol Sound."

Certainly, the Coach House was not the first place that Massive worked through their ideas—it did not open until 1989, and crucial sections of *Blue Lines* itself were hammered out at Cherry's and Cameron McVey's place in London, and in nearby studios there such as the famed Abbey Road. And, of course, the faction of the Wild Bunch that became Massive produced their first official release "Any Love" at the Smith & Mighty studio as early as 1988. That song featured falsetto vocals by a local singer named

Carlton, its chorus harmonized into a smooth R&B that was of a piece with Nellee Hooper's London-based Soul II Soul project back—a group famed for their alluring 1989 club classic "Back to Life."[1]

Ray Mighty remembers the "Any Love" session as the beginning of the Massive Attack idea. It was something that Marshall wanted to get off the ground, that Del Naja was thinking of in the mold of Afrika Bambaataa's Zulu Nation project: a hip-hop crew who traded rhymes over electro synths, funk guitars, and crisp drum machine beats. According to Mighty, Marshall showed up with several records to give a sense of the beat and a general sketch of the track. Although he was a reputed DJ, he was not yet a producer. Of the time, Marshall remembers, "[we were] not archetypal musicians. We're coming from the musical fan perspective . . . we got our chance to go to the studio from the aesthetics of hip-hop, we copied that sort of way of producing our music at first. That was our inroads, rather than being the Beatles."[2]

But Smith & Mighty had the infrastructure, and the experience working on records like their own version of "Anyone." They had also assembled their own two-room apartment-based studio. More DIY than professionally realized—they were doing the subtle work of monitoring recordings with unwieldy speaker cabinets—the duo had also begun to experiment with the rudimentary tape-based samplers of the era. And since their band days they had acquired some vital equipment: a Roland TR-606 drum machine, a TB-303 bass sequencer, and a KORG Poly 61 keyboard-style synth. In other words, Smith & Mighty had amassed the tools that were synonymous with the underground house, techno, and hip-hop records of the day, from the sharp, posthuman snap of the 606 to the acid house squelch of the 303. They also had the ability to sample and loop beats from existing records and to build songs by feeding phrases back into an eight-track recorder. But "Any Love," the initial outing under the aegis of "the Massive Attack," was in many respects a one-off. Carlton went his own way, and Smith & Mighty went on to their own iconic projects.

Del Naja has recalled that the origins of the Wild Bunch, as it moved from the Dugout to the multimedia performance of the hip-hop-inflected sound system, were partially a consequence of their lack of cash and proper instruments. But the tools on hand at Smith & Mighty's studio suggested a different approach. Suddenly, they were no longer just spinning records and rhyming, but creating entirely new tracks using a home-brew studio. As in other quarters of the digital underground, the bleeping boxes on hand were being used against the grain—in companies like Roland's estimation, this was meant to be ancillary gear that made it easy for pro musicians to practice in the bedroom or on the road, to noodle around and make rough sketches. But these devices were responsible for a wholly new sound; and access to this sort of setup provided a crucial entree for Massive, priming them for the opportunities that came with the full studio setup at The Coach House. "Technology has changed everything we've done," Del Naja observes. "Think back to the first primitive samplers we first picked up or the first keyboards to what you can do now. You sort of had to go out and record back in the day, you didn't have a choice. Now you can do it all on the laptop."[3]

*****

Andy Allan is a wiry builder raised in nearby Portishead. He studied to be an electrical engineer in the 1970s and had a sideline a decade later working for recording giant EMI, figuring out ways to push the data storage capacity of tape (an important question during those last days of the Soviet Union).[4] Allan lived for several years in south London, a classically trained musician who gigged as a fiddler, and sometimes lent his PA system to local punk bands. He returned to Bristol in 1980 with the hope of opening his own studio. After he found another musician, Bill Berrier, in a music store personal advert, the two went on to open The Cave. It went on to be the premier studio in Bristol until its closure in 1986.

The Cave was blessed by founders willing to invest heavily in the costly capital then necessary to run a pro studio, but it had its drawbacks. One was its "dead" room, a recording space that was flat, anechoic. As Allan points out, recordings are not simply instruments and microphones, but complex acoustic interactions with the rooms themselves, which subtly augment and inflect the sound on a record. In short, studios have a personality. This is, in no small measure, why artists like Dave Grohl of Foo Fighters have sought to preserve famed studios of the past fifty years, even celebrating them in documentaries.

A second problem was the neighborhood itself. St. Paul's was the epicenter of a few overlapping musical scenes and the rents were low. But in the aftermath of the uprisings there and throughout the country, the local council sought to invest in the area anew, which meant, among other things, developing some light industrial spaces as housing. Gentrification like this not only raises rents but brings new complications like noise complaints. By 1986, the Cave was forced out. Berrier cut loose, but Allan decided to double down, ultimately scouting a detached structure in the already established area of Clifton. It was, then as now, an inconspicuous out building that he ensured was airtight. No sound in, no sound out. He also installed a huge Soundcraft GB8 mixing board— dozens of channels, precise level control for catching subtle modulations in voicing and timbre, and plenty of room to loop effects, synths, and samples. In retrospect, this was akin to building England's best vacuum-tube computer five years before the birth of the Apple II. We all know the fate of the music industry at the dawn of the millennium.

But in its era, it was the product of exquisite thought and care. Like Mark Danielewski's famous "House of Leaves," the Coach House seems bigger on the inside than outside. Walking in, there is a mixing room off to the right, occupied by the board and, presently, by the guitars and effects pedals of current owner Tom Hackwell, a producer and leader of the rock band Armchair Committee. In recent years, he has revivified the studio for his own work, and other select projects.[5]

This mixing room has a lived-in feel, dotted with racks of instruments, piles of notes and books. Resting on the floor is a bizarre dynamo with heavy wiring: this is a variac, a quintessentially Andy Allan touch meant to dim the lights, creating ambiance without the signal interference from a traditional dimmer switch. And peering through the partition glass into the main room are the oddly angled wood panels that Allan long ago screwed into the wall. These are a mathematically randomized array of custom surfaces that were too reflective or absorbent. It's an acoustically neutral room that enables the capture of drums, reeded instruments, or voices. Long gone is a servo-driven ceiling that was MIDI-controlled—a reflective module that could be angled like a satellite to manipulate sound waves in the room in real time.

When they walked into this space, Massive Attack wasn't altogether different from the other local bands cutting their first demo-tapes, despite their long-established reputation as performers. Although gifted as subcultural impresarios, they were neither strong instrumentalists nor producers in the same way they are today. As Allan remembers, in those days before the DJ-cum-producer, groups like Massive were mostly one-off studio projects rather than road-tested bands or songwriting veterans. "It's at variance with people's cognitive dissonance that they want to believe this other story that they've made up, about all these guys, being the creative geniuses,"[6] Allan conceded. He points out that, especially in those days, Massive really was a collective in the sense of *Blue Lines* being a collaboration by many people. Pitching, tweaking, and refining ideas over time, the whole more than the sum of its parts.

This looseness also meant flexibility; it meant that individual contributions could come to the fore—a vocal stanza here, a synth line there—and iterate into something more. By most accounts, the producer Jonny Dollar, at the helm, was important in drawing these disparate threads together. He, like Rob Smith, had other important skills: in these early years of hip-hop and what became known as EDM, a vital turning point was the advent of sampling. This meant mastering a new technique, of selecting exactly which sections to pick out, elaborate, and recombine. According to Allan, "that's where the artistry came in. Whoever laid on top of that the melody, the vocal, the lyrics and all the rest. . . . There's a skill there in spotting the groove and making that properly . . . you can't just take any old loop and make it work. It takes a bit of intuition."

In those days, the studio was simple, tucked away in a glorified shed, but it was state-of-the-art and boasted an accumulation of AKG mics—precision tools used to capture classical instruments. Running many of these together through the big board, Allan and Jonny Dollar, who was twiddling the knobs there and back in London, were able to coax out and capture a broad and nuanced series of vocals and live fills that, as Hackwell argues, are "entwined" with the place itself. Where the technology did not exist, the people at the boards improvised, manipulating everything from effect returns to the tape-recording heads themselves.

Nonetheless, it's difficult to spell out exactly what went down at the Coach House during those fateful weeks in 1990 and 1991. With any record, much is lost to the sands of time, even the moments when all the key participants were lucid, and around to recall events down the line. By all accounts, the *Blue Lines* sessions were a loose affair, with members of the "collective" often in separate locations at separate intervals, joining up as needed to record a verse or plug away at a phrasing or a melody. Vowles often worked at home, and members of the group at times recorded independently. Even McVey and Dollar were unsure that a finished product would materialize from those sessions. It was far from inevitable that *Blue Lines* would emerge as the coherent whole that it is. Making the history of those session more complex still, several of the people in the room don't currently care to go down memory lane, citing it as a distraction or an episode from a distant past. The one person who could definitively tell the story, Jonny Dollar—the man who kept the wheels on the wagon—is no longer with us.

To complicate matters further, in spite of the legend of that studio as the Xanadu of trip-hop, there are merely three tracks that were recorded in their entirety there, and of those, only one mixed on site: "Lately," an unremarkable zenith before the soaring heights of the album closer, "Hymn of the Big Wheel." The latter track, like the iconic "Unfinished Sympathy," was sketched out at the Coach House, but cobbled together in London, with the addition of the orchestral finishes that lend both songs an epic quality.

In the absence of historical record, though, perhaps we can infer some things just by listening. What, after all, connects the Coach House tracks—"Safe from Harm," "One Love," and "Lately"? Two things: a simplicity of construction, mostly samples, looped and layered, with seamless overlays of bits and bobs of live drums; and the finest vocal performances on the record. In short, if *Blue Lines* is reduced down to its Coach House tracks, it sounds like a showcase for Shara Nelson, Horace Andy, and their producer. "One Love" is telling in this way. By today's standards, it's the model of simplicity with its drum machine beat, barely-there bass throb, and iconic electric piano—purloined from a lengthier Mahavishnu Orchestra workout—which has been looped to sound like a hammered guitar riff. The sequence is punched up by quiet little note bend here, a chugging horn sample (the opener to Isaac Hayes's "Ike's Mood") and record scratch there.

"One Love" is not complex. It could be a warm-up exercise on Garage Band. But, at the time, the track was an adept merger of new production techniques and a DJ's sense of how funk textures might interlock like puzzle pieces. A series of loose referents were conjoined into a concise jam oozing atmosphere and propelled by the snap of the snare drum. This song suggests that things were kept simple in the Coach House, that the key players turned up with samples and synths in mind. Little live details like a gentle piano outro or occasional kick drum could be recorded on the go. "One Love" also contrasts nicely with the titular "Blue Lines," which follows it. That song was realized at Eastcote Studio in London, and it is more complexly layered, jazzier, more in tune with the New Jack Swing and Native Tongues-styled records being made back in the United States. In short, "Blue Lines" the song simply has more going on—more vocal parts, more elements in the mix, more explicit conversation with then-contemporary music. From track 2 to track 3, one can practically feel the jump from one place to another, from the indies to the majors.

But more complex doesn't mean better. "Blue Lines" is head nodder, but "One Love" is iconic Massive Attack. It's sparse and strange and, importantly, showcases Horace

Andy in a wholly new context. It would change the course of his career, in much the way the film *Pulp Fiction* would, a few years later, change the way we saw veteran or washed-up actors through a new prism. Both the album and that film took motifs familiar to kids from the 1970s and mashed them up, viewed them through the knowing, if resourceful, "sample, remix, and recycle" ethos pioneered by producers throughout the 1980s. In "One Love" as on "Hymn of the Big Wheel," which was partially recorded in Bristol but post-produced to the extreme in London, Horace Andy's vocals cut through the mix, elevating the whole affair.

And this is, perhaps, what the Coach House did best for Massive Attack. As a studio suited to capturing the human voice, it drew out inflections and nuance in the delivery of all involved without compressing their range, without cooling them off. "Safe from Harm," the album opener, is perhaps best understood as a study in modulation. It was finished with ghostly whooshes and a dose of reverb, but it paired rasped or whispered stanzas of rhymes with Nelson's searing diva hooks. Those hooks are almost certainly the product of that idiosyncratic "main room" of the Coach House. Indeed, Allan seems to have built a purpose-made vocal booth (perhaps a former closet or powder room), which would have reduced ambient noise to produce a "clean vocal." This is a pro move, yet for the *Blue Lines* sessions, it sounds as though this room was sidestepped. The bigger, warmer, "dirtier" room was miked instead to capture not only vocal utterances but their interaction with real space—a neat analogy for the group itself.

Tom Hackwell has been able to reverse-engineer this effect some thirty years on, the conditions of what he notes is a "lovely, airy" vocal by Nelson. He set up condenser mics in a standard way (a few inches from the singer) and blended it with another mic some five feet away . . . space, texture, depth ensue. At two instances later in the "Safe from Harm," the drum line—sampled from Billy Cobham's "Stratus"— is punched up with a live kit—again, likely not recorded at the drums and cymbals themselves, but with elevated microphones aimed at the walls, to capture the sound reflecting from the Coach House itself. Thanks to "Safe from Harm," *Blue Lines* announces its force, its deftness from the opening bars. It's a song that sounds like the future, at once "massive" and ethereal, epic and intimate.

In short, the Coach House provided a laboratory in which the new sounds for which *Blue Lines* is credited could be devised and committed to tape. This was true in the basic sense of Massive making the transition from Smith & Mighty's place or Neneh Cherry's house to a full-on studio setup, one in which the technology was perfectly suited to the project. Not only could the studio handle the then-novel blending of all-programmed or sampled drums with live vocals and instruments, it could do so without sacrificing quality. But more generally, the Coach House engendered a sense of exploration. Any artist knows that it's one thing to be struck by inspiration, but quite another to have the tools to realize those ideas, or collaborators to hone them. By all accounts, the Coach House during those first years of the 1990s was home to a creative perfect storm. In Allan's estimation, what made the place special "was people's mental attitudes, and the fact they felt they were in a great environment, and they were able to produce the performances they did, and come up with the ideas they did. In the Coach House, there are no technical limits."

*****

In 1994, *Blue Lines* then *Protection* had skyrocketed to mainstream success, and it looked like an infinite horizon for Bristol and for the Coach House. The West of England was blowing up with media coverage, and there was a larger British Invasion underway from pop-music to the movies to the art world. The economy had also roared back to life and England was unquestionably cool again. Around this time, the BBC was granting extended leases on their auxiliary properties. Back in the days of the Blitz, it had made sense to decentralize the national airwaves, all the better to avoid a knockout blow by German planes. Fifty years on, they were ready to move on from Bristol's Christ Church, which as the name suggests was an epic facility in an actual church well before Arcade Fire made churches cool in the late 2000s. Allan took the lease, and even built out a custom facility for Massive Attack, who used the space for *Mezzanine*.

But the story of Allan and the Coach House starts to unravel there. High interest rates, long-term leases, and massive start-up costs collided with the next recession and the rise of newer digital technologies still—file sharing and portability that weaned millennials off of paying real money for beautifully recorded music. As Y2K neared, the Coach

House diminished, and Allan threw in the towel. His memory of the studio is bittersweet: "To get from where I was to the Coach House, that's ten years' hard graft . . . and living in penury to achieve it. The fact that something actually came out of it with international acclaim was a big reward for me."

But, it must have been quite a scene in the moment—the original studio up and running, all those people crammed under the low ceilings and dim lights. Dollar running the show, Allan hacking together new technical fixes and working as tape op, Shara Nelson and Horace Andy cutting virtuosic choruses, Marshall and Vowles chopping up the beats, and Del Naja trading verses with Tricky. Of course, there was another, then-unknown talent in the room. The "tea boy" on those sessions was a young turk named Geoff Barrow, who had previously applied through a government employment grant to work with Allan on a mobile recording setup and help build the studio. Several years later, Barrow would record Portishead's now-classic debut there and in nearby Bath. *Dummy*, too, was an example of a lushly realized hybrid of old and new—hip-hop breaks and electronic grooves animated by minor key guitars, pulsing bass, and lachrymose torch songs.

While it's easy for music critics to debate to what degree *Blue Lines* is a Bristol record, or what the Bristol sound actually was, there's an important material and social history here that can't be ignored. Masterpieces aren't made in a vacuum, and Massive's debut record bears the undeniable imprint of a few hundred square meters of real estate in that city—a studio where *Blue Lines* gestated and evolved, a studio that manifested the tenacity, energy, and innovation of other

Bristolians still, who are less remembered by posterity. For all that, like the group itself, the record was something of a Venn diagram, each track a confluence of disparate ingredients. As should be clear by now, the rest of this story runs through the big cities of London and New York. But, for now, we need to take one more detour through the byways of the West.

4
The Tricky Kid

This is a book that, in practice, is about Bristol. But it is not exactly about the "Bristol Sound." It's a truism of art or music criticism that writers need to find angles, to coin smart-sounding neologisms, isolate new circles of creative people, and then write articles and books about them. Almost universally, the artists in question shrug off these journalistic buzzwords, which, like neighborhoods made up to sell real estate, have an unfortunate way of sticking anyway. If this is true for artists and critics in general, it's particularly true for Bristolians, many of whom had zero interest in commenting for this book on the grounds that they were colonized by droves of opportunistic writers in the 1990s, and then forgotten.

Writers, it seems, are too often interested in dredging up the past rather than noting a vibrant present. And by the mid-1990s the bonanza to be had was figuring out "what was in the water" in Bristol. The next chapter takes up the problem of trip-hop as such, the umbrella under which the early 1990s coverage tended to fall, and one that conflated the markedly different sounds of Portishead, Massive, and one Adrian Thaws, known to the world as Tricky.[1] Indeed, if you know nothing else about *Blue Lines*, if you are a post-*Mezzanine* partisan, if you care not at all about British music as such but had a pulse during the 1990s, know this: in 1991, Massive Attack gave the world the Tricky Kid.

Tricky, for all his specificity and idiosyncrasy, was an undeniably crucial force *Blue Lines*, and kicked open the door to a solo career along the way. He is integral, for instance, to the hypnotic "Daydreaming," a song that is, in many ways, a rather pure distillation of the Massive sound. Musically, it is built around an iconic beat, and a sample of the first sections of Beninois composer Wally Badarou's instrumental "Mambo" from 1984. It's all atmospheric washes of keys and airy piano fills over a loping, expressive percussion. This is something of the effect DJ Snake would aim for thirty years later—funky and low BPM and vaguely western African. To listen to the full cut, it's unsurprising that Badarou actively collaborated with a who's who of unmistakably cool contemporaries, from Talking Heads to Herbie Hancock and Fela Kuti. Massive and Jonny Dollar cut the cheesier jazz-fusion excesses of the original but kept some of the shorter phrases of spooky dissonance. The track conveys a sense of hibernal interiority, its tones bordering on the occult. The lyrics here suggest otherworldly excursions, the hook intoning, "Well I'm floating on air when I'm daydreaming. . . ." Even the music video is made to maximize the eeriness—a tarot reader at the table, and a live scorpion on the prowl.

"Daydreaming"'s verses seem sutured into the beat, rather than merely riding atop it, and the overall sonic effect underscores the song's somnambulant message. Here Del

Naja and Tricky trade whispered, near-narcotized delivery. This is Tricky's self-declaration to a wider world: "Attitude is cool degrees below zero/Up against the wall behaving like De Niro/Tricky's performing taking his phono/Making a stand with a tan touch it like cocoa." It's a careful balance, invoking an auteurish vision of the alienated urban outlaw, but also insisting on a different tonality. He is black and tan, decidedly British but something else, something outernational. His languid meter and delivery signal that Tricky is not set on disruption so much as seduction . . . keeping it smooth, he suggests, with the record running steady, minute-by-minute, and deep in the groove. By the end of "Daydreaming," one has the sense of having been party to a kind of incantation, an initiation into both a tangible place beyond the veil and an abstract terrain of diaristic interiority. Tricky takes the listener on a journey to another plane.

As of 1995, Tricky had gone solo, having contributed to both *Blue Lines* and its follow-up, *Protection*, and, apparently, pressing up vinyl of his own tracks, such as "Aftermath" in parallel with his work with Massive. This led up to the languorous duet that was *Maxinquaye* in the late winter of that year. On its release, he was nominated as the latest avatar of Bristol alchemy. Dele Fadele's review of the record starts by musing that every

> few years, Bristol swims into focus once again as a hotbed of British musical talent, a happening place that throws up beguiling, poignant or just plain angry records . . . 1995 is belatedly shaping up to be the year of Massive Attack, Portishead and—most of all—Tricky. But you

have to be astute enough to catch them while you can, before they once again vanish.[2]

It's an alluring formulation. In contrast to the saturation bombing of other pop acts, the insistent hit production and making the rounds in celebrity publications, it sounds as if the Bristolians evanesce in and out of view, like fata morgana.

The *NME* review plainly gets a few things wrong. For one, it attributes the alternately spectral and sultry croon of Tricky's collaborator, the then-nineteen-year-old Martina Topley-Bird to someone named "Maxine." (In fact, Maxine was Tricky's mother, who died when he was young, and for whom the record is named.) But it does get other points bang on—the sensitivity, the sonic and poetic gender-bending, the disorienting construction of beats from sonic flotsam that (although Fadele doesn't go this far) invokes the haunted maritime shoals of a city built on slavery. The next bit of the review also gives the lie to the conceit of a unified regional identity. He remarks that

> Tricky Kid is one of Bristol's least definable sons . . . a rapper who made his name by contributing to Massive Attack's "*Blue Lines.*" Now he's gone right off the map with no compass to bring you . . . an LP with no precedents, blueprints or antecedents. You never know what's going to happen next and you're not quite sure what you're taking in . . . yet you're held spellbound, enraptured, lost at the edge of words. . . .

That's about as good a description of *Maxinquaye* as has ever been written, and it describes in real time what it felt like to queue that record up and listen to it in full, a psychotropic excursion that feels a bit like taking the red pill and wondering where you'll wind up. If *Blue Lines* is a new form of postcolonial soul record, one pitched toward private, nocturnal explorations, *Maxinquaye* is a full-on journey into hell (albeit an elegant and artful one). To this extent, Tricky's music quickly became useful for more cinematic purposes, framing scenes redolent of dark energy, as in the reedy opening bars of "Overcome" in Ralph Fiennes's tense cyber-snuff film *Strange Days* (1995). That movie—a fascinating primary source in its own right—took a collective barometric reading, registering what is by now a scarcely believable anxiety, echoed in media and pop culture both, about the coming turn of the century. And Tricky, too, would name his third record *Pre-Millennium Tension*.

While Tricky and Bird's delivery throughout *Maxinquaye* is languid and intimate, the record as the whole registers like the sonic equivalent to another film from that year, David Fincher's captivating procedural *Seven*. Which is to say, for all of its psychotropic beauty, *Maxinquaye*'s interior spaces exude a sense of danger. Around every corner, a haunted music box chimes. Fragments of the soul that animate *Blue Lines* here lull you into a Shangri-La of dim lanterns and piled carpets where someone declares they will "fuck you in the ass" (and not in a good way). Part of the uncanniness of listening to *Maxinquaye* at the time was a sense that you had been there before—an effect drawn into sharper relief in the age of Spotify, where curated playlists of trip-hop place 1995-era records side by side. That is, Tricky was already at work sampling himself and drawing laterally from his Bristol peers. "Overcome" echoes Massive's "Karmacoma," and he includes a veritable remake of Portishead's "Glory Box" from their iconic record *Dummy*. Both "covers" plainly reference the originals, but warp them, take them onto a darker ground, away from the comforting shores of reggae jams or jazz standards.

Such transfiguration is most notable in Tricky's cover of Public Enemy's 1988 "Black Steel in the Hour of Chaos." Chuck D's original rhymes are seemingly a nod to the Vietnam War draft, detailing the hypocrisy of conscripting black people. The Public Enemy release, with its trippy piano and stuttering beat, marked the seriousness of the group's political address. They positioned their music as an extension of a deeper vein of black activism in the United States. It was a throwing down of the gauntlet to be sure, but also decidedly a hip-hop record, complete with record scratches and driven by Chuck D's percussive, deliberate basso. But Tricky's version blurs the lines, inverts the formula on a few levels.

In the *Maxinquaye* update, Chuck D's vocal is replaced by Martina's serpentine contralto and the beat sped up to a frantic drum'n'bass awash in psychedelic squalls and thrash guitar, all filtered to sound like it's being played through the afterburner of a jet engine. Both versions of the song call out to a wide palette of American history, from fugitive slaves to Malcolm X's invocation of white devilry. But Tricky's cover expands the purview of the words. The act of covering "Black Steel" itself suggests a sense of solidarity with other diasporic people, those brought to Europe and the United States through the channels of slavery and colonialism.

And, in the context of 1990s England, Tricky's use of Chuck D's words sketch an important symmetry: between two governments founded on fundamental rights but had failed their immigrant communities decade after decade.

In the years following *Maxinquaye*, Tricky moved to New York, seeking local collaborations and serving as something of an ambassador. While there are some clear instances of overlap between Massive Attack and New York–based rappers (e.g., "Mushroom" Vowles's work with early 1980s hip-hop legends the Fearless Four), the group essentially took inspiration from and translated the American scene from afar, creating an admixture with sounds more ambient in Bristol. Accordingly, the hip-hop press in the United States—in those days not always attuned even to the various Southern and Western regionalisms in the domestic scene—did not readily see Massive peers. For mainstream hip-hop audiences, Massive barely registered and were taken up by fans of independent rock and a burgeoning electronic mainstream within the United Kingdom. According to journalist Michael Gonzalez, however, Tricky was another story. He recalls that "the person in the trip-hop world that really made the [hip-hop] connection clearer was Tricky, simply because he came to New York and worked with the rap crews. Tricky was remaking Public Enemy, recording with Gang Starr's label Pay Day, working with Rza, remixing Biggie's 'Hypnotize' and touring (briefly) with Jeru the Damaja."[3]

There were other obvious resonances still. Tricky hailed from Knowle West, a working-class Council Estate, a marginal place in a then-peripheral city. And that sense of place suffused his work then and now, with solo record titles like *Mixed Race* and *Knowle West Boy*. He grew up in a tightly knit community south of the Bath Road, a few miles outside of Bristol. Which is to say, unlike his bandmates, he was from the projects, socially and spatially removed from "downtown." He describes Knowle West as a "white ghetto" where it's "about your family's name and not what color you are. . . . We didn't go to school much. My grandmother used to sing, my grandad played the washboard with thimbles and whistling, so I grew up listening to prison songs and prison stories. So if there's any questions about why my music's dark, it's pretty obvious."[4]

Joining up with the Wild Bunch in his late teens may have saved Tricky's life. By 17 he had been jailed for stealing bank notes, and as he describes in an interview, his brother may be able to handle prison life, but not so for him.[5] While this admission shows that Tricky doesn't embody the fraught persona of the American gangster rapper, he is a liminal figure all the same—of mixed racial descent, partial to wistful stories of his white grandfathers that conform to an outlaw narrative. He describes them as a notorious family of street fighters, horse dealers, and suave gangsters, what he calls the original Knowle Westers, "hardworking families and also hard criminal families." In this sense, Tricky's own upbringing rang true back in New York, where the hip-hop of the day was notable for its urban storytelling, its rappers representing disenfranchised communities of color (like the various projects of Brooklyn and Queens), often borrowing from the hardboiled genres of organized crime and the Wild West. There was a symmetry in background and sensibility shared by Tricky and American peers like Nas or the Wu Tang Clan not necessarily shared among the wider collective that was Massive Attack.

But even the most catholic of samplers, pop-culture junkies, and name checkers in the New York scene could not quite match Tricky, who had clear auteurist sensibilities and a range of influences that surpassed the outer limits of the hip-hop of the day. One could hear Caribbean patois and dolorous string arrangements in the offerings of Busta Rhymes, or loving references to chop socky films and Eastern spiritualism in the work of RZA and company. For his part, Tricky not only dropped lyrical nods to his influences but also worked them into the fibers of the music itself. His mid-1990s work, routed through hip-hop as it might have been, simply defied genre. In one sense, his protean nature was not merely musical, but existential, what might now be called queer—an insistence on deforming boundaries and resisting binaries.

Linguistically dextrous, wont to wear dresses, Tricky was ultimately less a British counterpart to his collaborators in the United States. He was more akin to David Bowie, who was himself experimenting with the harder edges of industrial music production at the time. Tellingly, Tricky remembers sitting in bed, listening to the sylvan chanteuse Kate Bush, thinking, "when I listen to music, I always want to be that artist . . . one day I realized I could be Kate Bush, I could be the Specials, I could be Gary Newman, I could be whatever I want. . . . You can probably hear it in my music—I'm a wannabe. I want to be a tough guy, a rapper, a girl."[6] Which is to say, some twenty-five years before Drake or Frank Ocean made sensitivity or sexuality a more fluid terrain to be explored in hip-hop, Tricky was encoding it into productions that risked failure but ventured into the unknown. Indeed, when *Vibe* profiled Tricky in 1995, they depicted a "hardcore" MC boasting a typical rags-to-riches story: he "had to be brought back from near death after an excess of cocaine. He's a rapper now." But the piece concludes with a blunt counterpoint, in which he declares, "In Britain, if you're a black man you do reggae, soul, rap—I'm saying, Nah, I do anything I want. . . . A black man ain't supposed to be involved with thrash music, or look certain ways, but I'm saying, fuck what you think."[7]

Unsurprisingly, this boundary-crossing spirit took on metaphysical tones as well. Tricky will not be confined to the humdrum of everyday life. And his very nom-de-guerre suggests a refusal to be pinned down, an invocation of a whole litany a "trickster" figures, from Shakespeare's Ariel to the afro-diasporic orishas, such as Eshu, the god of creative energy and the crossroads. This mutability, so plain in his music, once inspired Bowie himself to pen an "imagined" conversation with Tricky—in this telling a specter, a folk hero protected by the hardscrabble locals. He wrote that "I'd been chasing Tricky for a number of weeks, diving down into the low bars of Bristol. . . . He's been spied by the Magpie girl only last Thursday, slipping in and out of the shadows down by the quay, drawing black lines on his own posters drenched in salty-sea splash, grinning synergy and singing swatches of malodorous song."[8]

And it's fair to say that much of Tricky's contribution to Massive Attack early on was a sense of otherworldly influence, from that Tarot deck reader in the "Daydreaming" video—probably not his suggestion, but fitting—or casual references in "Blue Lines" to being raised English but "background Caribbean." (Tricky seems to own the persona of the mystic in interviews—more on that later.) He is the introspective one here, already meditating on the multiaccentuality of his identity, already gazing outward into dreamworlds and other dimensions, his ego doubled, unstable: "It's a beautiful day well, it seems as such/Beautiful thoughts means I dream too much/Even if I told you, you still would not know me/Tricky never does, Adrian mostly gets lonely."

But as singular as Tricky's approach is, he is part of a venerable tradition.[9] If much black music is already rooted in African inheritances—the syncopation of jazz and the breakbeat, the call and response of gospel and hip-hop—from the 1960s forward latent tendencies toward the ghostly and otherworldly began to manifest even more clearly. This is especially true of dub and reggae, and in the hybrid variants that began to emerge in the early 1990s. Think of the eerie cinematic productions of the Black Audio Film collective, the gothic accounts of Dr. Octagon and the Gravediggas, or the reverb-soaked, bass-infused influences on which records by the Fugees and Roots Manuva were built. These last projects, one made in New York, the other in London, share so many symmetries that they more or less illustrate the academic theory of the "Black Atlantic." It was Roots Manuva, not Tricky, that might claim the mantle of inventing a truly British hip-hop, the influence of which can be heard from figures as diverse as Dizzee Rascal to Wiley and even King Krule.

For his part, Tricky probably found a Bristolian precursor to his own productions in Smith & Mighty, their long-delayed debut *Bass is Maternal* setting the tone for dub/punk fusions of the era. It is a palette suffused with otherworldly echoes and distorted instrumentation and orchestration. But then, the influence question is perhaps moot in the case of Tricky: clearly porous to his environment, he is an absorptive synthesizer and reinventor. It's not quite clear whether his career would not have been possible without his peers or vice versa. Certainly, there is a clear demarcation between Tricky's two records with Massive and those that came after his departure and in the tailwinds of *Maxinquaye*. He was, in hindsight, deeply attuned to his own internal oscilloscope, reading invisible currents in the energetic field. His second record was released under the pseudonym Nearly God. In the lead single "I be Prophet," he experiments with genre-less spoken word and string arrangement. The track sounds like an Aphex Twin outtake and alludes to a sense of messianic self-certainty.

Similarly, "Christiansands" from the official sophomore outing *Pre-Millennium Tension* begins with one of the most recognizable phrases of this entire complex of "Bristol records," just a brief repeating guitar line. (Go ahead, listen online, you'll recognize it.) But then the throbbing sub-bass drops and does not relent. Tricky's vocals here are a raspy whisper somehow amplified but run through a ragged filter, like a transmission on an interdimensional transistor radio: "I met a Christian in Christiansands, a devil in Helsinki." Kristiansand, like Helsinki, is a coastal Scandinavian city, alternately drenched in endless summer or drowned in darkness, but here they figure in something of a biblical parable, one part Robert Johnson selling his soul at the crossroads, one part Saul of Tarsus falling from his horse.

Tricky's mystical enthusiasm and mutable personality come through in conversations from the period. Simon Reynolds recalls interviewing him during the press tour for *Nearly God*.[10] Perhaps unsurprisingly, Reynolds learns of his upbringing by his maternal grandmother, who used to stare at him incessantly, believing him to be a reincarnated version of his deceased mother. Less surprisingly still, Tricky recorded the entire *Nearly God* record in New York over the course of a few days off. He smokes four joints during the interview, musing that he had been to see a psychic because he found himself "wearing loads of silver." He said, "the psychic woman told me it symbolizes Mercury, the messenger God. She gives you a massage and each different muscle tells different stories. She wrote that I came to this Earth too quick, I wasn't ready, but I said 'Fuck it, c'mon, let's go. . . . Mad, innit?'"

It's that sense of openness to the murmurings of the universe, and to his own inner compass, that comes through so clearly on *Blue Lines*. His voice bends and syncopates through his verses—a kind of working-class griot amid Del Naja's hushed delivery and Marshall's ragga-style baritone. If the Wild Bunch were outward looking, taking in data from the States, Asia, the Continent, Tricky was tuned into different frequencies, idiosyncratic ones that emanated from an introspective certitude. Many critics have described *Blue Lines* as headphone hip-hop, slowed down moon music for darkened bedroom listening. And for all the cacophony and darkness of later records like *Mezzanine*, the first two records—those featuring Tricky—mine a different kind of interiority. Del Naja puts it well in "Daydreaming," commenting that he's "living in his headphones." One can image him, imagine Tricky meandering down the street on a drizzling day, past the Council Estate blocks, amid the grandeur and ghosts of Clifton or, later, on jets in unfamiliar cities, cocooned in their own psychic membrane. One foot here, one foot elsewhere.

In this sense, *Blue Lines* laid the groundwork for a distinctively British form of hip-hop, one rooted in Caribbean sonic sensibilities (also integral to its Bronx foundations, in the person of Kool Herc and the sound system model), but that played out on a parallel path. To that foundation Massive and Tricky added lyrics and flow suited to the more housebound and headphone-clad sensibilities of life on the Avon. They looked in two directions, outward to the specific racial and class dynamics of 1980s England, and inward to more psychedelic and transcendental realms rarely alighted on back in the States. Meanwhile, MCs like Roots Manuva and producers like Roni Size and DJ Krust took up the mantle of black music formed in dialogue with the wider world but still decidedly British. At the same time, Tricky sloughed off the confines of genre altogether even as Massive began to forge what would become their signature aesthetic by decade's end—a move that confounded the neat categories of the record industry and music press, heralding the birth of something new.

Interlude
Living in My Headphones

The book in your hands was pitched to the publisher several years ago. One of the hooks in that pitch was that in recording *Blue Lines*, Massive Attack more or less invented trip-hop, a genre that defined much of the decade to follow. At the same time, Massive would, like most Bristol musicians of a certain generation, probably gladly never hear this term again. Ever.

Music critic Simon Reynolds covered Massive Attack early on as a member of the British rock press. In 1998, he argued that "musicians, bless 'em, hate categories. 'Don't pigeonhole us.' . . . In recent years, no genre designation has been more resented and rejected as a press-connoted figment by its purported practitioners than 'trip-hop.'" This preamble is from Reynolds's encomium of underground dance music *Energy Flash*, initially published somewhat midstream in 1998, seven years after *Blue Lines*'s release. By then, he concluded that the term "trip-hop," allegedly coined by Mixmag's Andy Pemberton, "instantly evokes what it describes: a spacey, down-tempo form of hip hop that's mostly abstract and all instrumental," with Massive Attack "widely regarded as the genre's inventors."[1]

Bearing all that in mind, when dedicating an entire book to a record, it'd be irresponsible not to take the commonsense understanding of the thing at face value. Mea culpa: what follows, while arguably necessary, partakes of the same critical nitpicking and self-seriousness that, at various moments, it seeks to document or make light of. If this is not your thing, you can skip ahead and pick up the story of *Blue Lines*. For now, a brief, critical digression.

Is there such a thing as trip-hop? Most serious fans of 1990s music probably think so. In those pre-Napster days, listeners still lived, by and large, at the whim of a still-thriving and seemingly monolithic system of music distribution—major labels, TRL on MTV, and buying records at Tower or the Virgin Store. That system sought to commodify subcultural and indie sounds—pioneered by a loose, if fervent rebel alliance—by charting new formats, creating new headers in local CD bins. On one hand, the term specifies essentially nothing: to get a sense of "trippy hip-hop," you'd have to agree on what hip-hop is on a kind of existential level, or at least what constituted hip-hop during the early 1990s. And what of the "trip" part? Is that to do with electronic music, and if so, would that be disco-inflected strains of house music? The bleeps and bloops of techno? The bro-down excesses and Balearic vibes of UK Acid? In 1998, Reynolds hypothesizes a hybridization of hip-hop and rave culture possible in the United Kingdom, but not possible in the United States, where genres were kept to their respective corners.

On the whole, trip-hop is a portmanteau perfectly suited to a decade that saw the conjoining of truly disparate kinds of music under reductive marketing schemes—Bush and Nirvana and Silverchair all jostling under the banner of "grunge," or the truly hardcore (go ahead, listen again) and massively popular recordings of Liam Howlett and the Prodigy filed alongside the louche analog grooves of the Gallic duo Air as "electronica." At the same time, the mid-1990s were perhaps the golden age (if not the high watermark) of music snobbery, as Gen-Xers parlayed their fresh humanities graduate degrees into rarefied analyses of popular culture. Childhood nostalgia could be tarted up or talked to death using Derridean deconstruction while waiting in line for a burrito, and audiences thrilled to resolute slackers waxing intellectual about the ethics of the Death Star in movies such as Kevin Smith's *Clerks* (1994).[2]

The musical corollary to Smith's slacker suburbia, of course, was the independent record shop, a place of hazing and initiation chronicled in loving detail by Nick Hornby in *High Fidelity* (1995) and its adaptation by Stephen Frears in 2000. John Cusack's character Rob, in this version, owns a barely-above-water record shop called Championship Vinyl, which is one part clubhouse and one part seminar room, home to troves of Japanese-imports and original pressings, walls papered with stickers for British dance music labels. It has a punk section, and one for salsa and soul and neoromantic records and, of course, one for trip-hop. The clerks who run Championship are sure to underscore this point—that they have a trip-hop section. And when Cusack's Rob is naming off his all-time top-five first tracks on first sides of a record, he cites the Velvet Underground and, yes, Nirvana, but also drops in "Radiation Ruling the Nation,"

London dub producer Mad Professor's instrumental remix of Massive's 1994 hit "Protection."

There are two takeaways here. One is that records like *Blue Lines* defied category even as hip-hop was shifting away from its explicitly political ambitions and toward a more unified culture industry centered on urban American cultural identity, with its own founding myths. As the cultural critic and "Notorious Ph.D.," Todd Boyd has noted, hip-hop was both more commercialized and more unified than ever as the 1990s began. This was done at the cost of much of its visionary and open-ended challenges of the status quo, and by placing identity and "authenticity" at the forefront.[3] In short, there was little room for the likes of Massive Attack or Tricky at the very instant of *Blue Lines*'s release. Official outlets, like *Source* or *Vibe*, or the reams of emerging hip-hop scholarship scarcely touched on the American MCs' transatlantic cousins. A related point, then, is that heterodox forms of hip-hop lacked "authenticity" and would have to be received by a different public, and under a distinct aegis. *Blue Lines* was a seriously cool record for the rock and dance press; less so for the hip-hop and jazz worlds with which it arguably had far more in common. That is, you would have bought your copy at "Championship Vinyl" in a neighborhood like Wicker Park, Camden, or the East Village.[4]

The problem here is that "trip-hop" is the way that rock journalists and indie record enthusiasts talk about Massive Attack, but not the way Massive Attack talked about themselves. More to the point, in contrast to the ardent fanboys and keepers of the citadel, the actual music was being made by producers like Massive, or Tim Goldsworthy and James Lavelle (cofounders, in various capacities, of Mo' Wax Records [1992], DFA Records, and UNKLE), or DJ Shadow, Luke Vibert, Amon Tobin, and many, many others. These producers, it's fair to say, would be right at home at Championship Vinyl—not navel gazing about minor gradations of genre but, instead, buying records from any and all bins. They'd be crate diving, rummaging, mining for overlooked gems.[5] To be sure, the samples on *Blue Lines* were deep cuts from the treasure troves of 1970s-era soul, funk, reggae, and jazz—not the sort of marquee Motown or rock 'n' roll stuff that everyone's folks had in their personal collection. Finding those samples was an act of volition, not just nostalgia.

But if it was anything at all, trip-hop was music that relied on sampling and breakbeats, music that was for and by producers (people who liked record stores) and less for MCs—especially MCs in the American model. Trip-hop merely specified, in commercial friendly terms, an emergent form of hip-hop-rooted composition that was fueled by a sense of aestheticism and eclecticism lacking, in say, west coast gangsta rap, which fused mid-1970s hits with blustery, reportage-style lyrics. Here's Reynolds again: in spite of atmospheric work by Mantronix or Erik B. and Rakim, with the politicized rappers of the late 1980s ascendant, in the United States, "the verbal, storytelling side of hip hop gradually came to dominate at the expense of aural atmospherics . . . [in contrast] hip hop's influence in the UK blossomed in the form of jungle and trip-hop, distinctly British mutants that Black Americans barely recognized as relatives of rap."[6]

A quick comparison that makes this point is the way in which the sounds of the 1970s were differently appropriated. A song like Dr. Dre's "Let Me Ride" or Diddy's "I'll be Missing You" takes a blockbuster track by Parliament or the Police and uses the riff and the vocal hook as the foundation for songs about driving around LA, for instance, or missing a departed friend. The genius, the resonance of those songs is that they were mixed atop immediately recognizable melodies taken more or less whole cloth from elsewhere. You might not connect with Puffy's flow, or know the story of Biggie Smalls, but anyone who's ever been to a Walgreens or waited in the lobby of a car wash knows the relentless thump of Sting's insidious bass line. Maybe you don't care about "rollin' in a '64," but try not to dance to P-Funk. While the opening years of the 1990s were marked by a broad cultural debate around the ethics and legality of sampling, as well as the "explicit lyrics" featured in so much "gangsta rap," a more salient criticism might be that such songs played it safe; they were surefire pop hits.[7]

Massive's strategy was markedly different. While they, too, relied on the power of post-production in the studio and the appropriation-friendly horizons of 1980s music, they operated on a more granular level, working under the vocal track with the assiduous subtlety of the remixer. And aside from some audience crossover, this is more or less where the "rave culture" comparison starts to lose steam. *Blue Lines*, for instance, featured a version of William De Vaughn's 1974 track "Be Thankful for What You Got," which is a lovely, if lesser known, paean to the virtues of gratitude. Indeed, it's fair to say that the message of this song is precisely the opposite of what was on offer in most American hip-hop, most of the time, for most of its history. To wit: "Though you may not drive a great big Cadillac/Gangster whitewalls TV antenna in the back/You may not have a car at all/But just remember brothers and sisters/You can still stand tall/Just be thankful for what you've got."

The original version of "Be Thankful" runs to just over seven minutes—it's languid, funky, with an insistent beat layered in the sumptuous instrumentation so typical of the era's studio productions. It's all there, the chiming electric organ, xylophone, tom-toms, finger snaps, and angular guitars down in the mix, chucka chucking away. This is the sort of song Daft Punk was trying to remake on *Random Access Memories*. The emerging (and soon-to-be standard), hip-hop move circa 1991 would be to sample off roughly four bars of the main guitar phrase, fatten up the beat, and let the MC lay down a few verses on whatever catches their fancy—endo, gin cocktails, personal vendettas, etc. Massive's version of "Be Thankful" is decidedly not that. No Daddy G or 3D rapping over the remnants of a soul classic. Instead, they produced what amounts to a thoughtful cover, but using production techniques suited to the hip-hop era.

For one, their version sounds like mediated analog. This is the re-recording of technological residues, the white noise, hisses, and pops that convey not just music but the sound of listening to pre-digital forms of music. Producers like Burial would later become known for this strategy, and "Be Thankful" uses the effect too. Like a photo of a photo, it conjures a record captured in playback, but augmented by subtle scratching and repetition. The drums, still full of tone, are tightened up and given some depth, the snare made less shambling, sharper. The total runtime of the song is pared down by three minutes—it's made to be sequenced into a record laid out in advance by a DJ, the first drum hit picking up seamlessly with the last measure of the previous track, "Blue Lines," and its loose, syncopated flow.

In Massive's version, the lyrics are essentially faithful to the original, rather than scrubbed away to make room for fresh verses. Instead, Tony Bryan was called in to lay down the vocals anew. Bryan is now known mostly for other one-offs from this period, including an electro-funk solo track called "Love is the Only Way," which in 1993 was remixed by a young Fatboy Slim and released on the Ultrasonic label.[8] Bryan was associated with the sort of records that sound so quintessentially 1992, equally at home alongside the New Jack Swing of Tony! Toni! Toné! or Keith Sweat. Bryan's cover is faithful, and his voice smoothly charts a middle path between Vaughn's classic soul intonation and Horace Andy's spectral croon. In the context of *Blue Lines*, the song is something of a homage, and one that signals a deeper lineage of influences through which the record should be understood. As a listening experience, it is akin to "Exchange" on the *Mezzanine* record, a druggy, doo-woppy interstitial and coda, a scratchy dispatch from an earlier era that also manages to cement the record as a unified aesthetic statement.

Which is to say, whatever trip-hop was, it was more urbane than grittily urban—its easy cosmopolitanism succinctly, coolly articulated in songs like "Be Thankful."

More generally, trip-hop in the Massive Attack mold is knowingly auteurish, but nonetheless indebted to a sample/remix/mash-up model central to a version of hip-hop beat composition. Importantly, though, Massive's projects drew overlapping, even concentric circles with that of the American producer DJ Shadow, whose 1996 breakthrough *Endtroducing* on the Mo' Wax label features a cover image of a black and an Asian man digging through the bins at a record store. Shadow's own version of an instrumental interstitial for his album is incredibly brief, at 42 seconds. But it is nonetheless immediately recognizable: a fusion of two samples, an electro-funk bass and keyboard line from "Snap" by Cleo McNett and a vocal snippet from a 1969 track by soul group Samson and Delilah. The spooky whole notes on the synth would have been generically familiar to most people in the mid-1990s—the sound of gansta-rap, of "g funk" (think Snoop Dogg or Warren G). The new song is called "Why Hip Hop Sucks in '96," and its vocal sample rings out an insistent, echoing "it's the money . . ."

"Why Hip Hop Sucks in '96," is, to be clear, a kind of "diss track" (albeit, in a year that saw the mainstream release of a track by Tupac Shakur that boasts of cuckolding Biggie Smalls and threatening to dismember his friends and family, a rather measured one). In fact, Shadow's call-out was probably so subtle in register that it may as well have been a dog whistle. But that was the point: he was putting a marker down for connoisseurship over posturing solipsism; craft and patience over commercial success; process over reward. In short, the mid-1990s were, it is now clear, the broader moment when hip-hop was not yet the lifeblood of pop music—full stop—but had already cleaved into more commercial and more purist or "backpack" variants.

Consider, for instance, pioneering hip-hop producer Afrika Bambaataa, he of the electro-funk synths and chants of Zulu nation, back when hip-hop was in its primordial soup days, not yet fully formed as a defined set of cultural tropes. His project at the dawn of the 1980s was one of explicit activism and cultural uplift, centered on the daily lives of people in the Bronx. By 1999 Bambaataa was an unfamiliar name to mainstream hip-hop audiences in the United States. Yet he was working on a track called "Africa Shox" that became a landmark for dance DJs the world over. His production partners? Not Diddy, or Timbaland, or Kanye. He was pushing genre boundaries yet again, penning a song with the (white) British duo Leftfield, already known for an earlier collaboration with John Lydon ("Open Up") that was featured alongside Massive's "Protection" on 1995's *Hackers* soundtrack.

With this background in mind, it's unsurprising that *Blue Lines* was not covered by the then-emerging hip-hop media. It's telling that twenty-five years later, *The Source* magazine seems to have no archival coverage of Massive's early work, but claims the 2016 record *Ritual Spirit* as a British/European album of the month. With the benefit of hindsight, this brief review cites *Blue Lines* and *Mezzanine* as "stone cold classics" that used "sampling and live instrumentation to create atmospheric, layered music [that] was completely alien upon release."[9]

But *Blue Lines* was, in so many ways, a hip-hop record—it relied on genre-defining techniques such as sampling and scratching. Many of its verses are unmistakably rapped rather than whispered or sung. The liner notes are sure to note sources of inspiration, including 1970s legends the Neville Brothers and Isaac Hayes, Golden Age[10] MCs Rakim and Marley Marl, and tough New York films like *Dog Day Afternoon* and *Taxi Driver*. Such shout outs would have been right at home on a Wu Tang Clan record, and the team behind *Blue Lines* seems to have incorporated the stylistic cues and downtown mythos of the Naked City itself into the album's very genetic code. And here's a recent *Pitchfork* review: when the record was recorded, "the sub-genre called trip-hop hadn't been invented. But at its heart, *Blue Lines* is a hip-hop record, although one marbled with streaks of soul, dub, dance music, and psychedelic rock. The fact that its primary audience in America was made up largely of ravers and alternative rockers doesn't change that."[11]

Nonetheless, in what was likely *Blue Lines*'s highest profile review on its release, Reynolds argues in the *New York Times* that Massive had made a major contribution to . . . psychedelic rock. The title of the review is a bit misleading, but Reynolds summarizes the novelty of Massive's sound by noting that although they use "house and hip-hop techniques like sampling, rapping and turntable-scratching, most of its songs are much slower than the club norm of 120 beats per minute; they range from about 90 beats per minute to a torpid 67. Dance records usually simulate the uproar of communal celebration, but Massive Attack's vibe is meditational rather than gregarious."[12] Another way of putting this is that while most hip-hop of the era was made explicitly for blasting from car stereos or banging away at the club, *Blue Lines* represented a shift toward records made for the lounge or the bedroom. This could be seen most closely in hip-hop terms through the work of, say, Digable Planets—fellow fans, like Massive, of Herbie Hancock. *Blue Lines*, in short, was a studio record through and through, and one that was pathbreaking on those very grounds. Reynolds's argument, at least at the time, was that the psychedelia of dance culture (embodied for him by Massive, Soul II Soul, and the KLF) had entered a prog-rock phase, one in which making concept records rather singles was suddenly possible.

Concept records, fans of Pink Floyd or Rush might recall, are made not for the dance floor, but for lighting a candle, pouring a drink and listening to the long play. More passively, one envisions such a record as being suitable for all sorts of interior pursuits, from meditative contemplation to making love, to walking the streets on a rainy afternoon. Interiority here is not just spatial, but a way of being that is accessible to anyone with a headset. This last point is particularly important: what Reynolds and others writing about *Blue Lines* have often pointed to as its studio triumph that it is perhaps best enjoyed while lying on the floor, head on a pillow, hi-fi (and maybe some acid) washing over the senses.

Robert Del Naja puts it even better, in the song "Daydreaming." He declares himself to be "Living in my headphones, Sony's what I say to 'em/The surreal boom of the Budokan stadium." Rock fans might recognize "Budokan" as the stadium built in Tokyo for the 1964 Olympics, which became a storied venue for acts ranging from Led Zeppelin to Cheap Trick to the Doobie Brothers. It's also a homonym for the Sony "Boodo Khan" (WM-DD100) Walkman, a unit released in 1987 and prized for its onboard EQ system and bass boost, and its bespoke DR-S3 DJ-style headphones, complete with iconic kanji lettering. Translation: this was a portable tape player made for an audiophile market, and its closed headphones allowed the listener to be cocooned in sound while on the move, ambling through the misty streets of Bristol, say. While professional-grade headphones (Beats, Bose, etc.) have more recently been popularized for a mass market, they would have stood out in the late 1980s. Budakhans were a statement of purpose. Their rich sound would, indeed, have created a dreamlike atmosphere, to allow one to ride on air as they made their way around town to, as Del Naja implores his "heavy" brothers, "get lighter than helium/Float above the world to break the tedium."

With *Blue Lines*, in other words, Massive left behind the world of mid-afternoon sound systems and—more generally—the world of singles, of dubplates, DJ battles, and DIY public performance. But is it a trip-hop record? Indeed, the wellspring of all trip-hop? In a sense, no, as Massive were part of a larger current of sophisticated, omnivorous repurposing of extant musical forms into something new. That something, in retrospect, evokes a certain introspective elegance, and seems part of a whole constellation of musicians working in the early 1990s. In a sense yes, because when we talk about trip-hop retrospectively, it's Exhibit A. But then, perhaps only in a sort of tautological way: trip-hop sounds like *Blue Lines* which sounds like trip-hop and so on.

A more interesting question than "is *Blue Lines* the first trip-hop record" is "how did transatlantic strains of hip-hop reconcile each other?" And how did that bizarre dialogue play out across the 1980s and 1990s? The answer is the work of at least a few books or podcasts. The preceding pages, for their part, give a partial answer. Still other ways into that conversation run right through histories of the London fashion world, through global graffiti and, in both cases, right back to Massive Attack.

5
The Cherry Bear Organization

Neneh Cherry's pitch-perfect 1989 "Buffalo Stance" video has it all: funky tambourines, hip-hop flappers, split screens, psychedelic fabrics . . . a man playing a tiny keyboard. It's also got a DJ with a gold tooth scratching records—could it be Andrew "Mushroom" Vowles? All this, and a singer telling cautionary tales about "gigolos." While that particular term for a "scrub" doesn't seem to have stuck, Cherry, the daughter of West African and Scandinavian parents and step-daughter of free jazz legend Don Cherry, was a nimble scanner of cultural codes. The boom years of her career—roughly 1989–1992—put her smack in the middle of an increasingly global hip-hop, post-Acid dance music, and high fashion. Like her contemporary Madonna, Cherry had her ear to the ground and surrounded herself with top flight producers.

The result was a kind of mash-up of sounds that you might expect from a singer who, in interviews from the time, described herself as an open-minded conduit, the music flowing through her on its own terms. But she was a singular messenger. Having spent the formative years of her late teens/early 1920s cutting her teeth in Clifton and the Bristol underground, she was informed by that city but not of it. In all of her innate and cultivated cosmopolitanism, she was in many ways the opposite of the guys from Massive.

Marshall recalls of that time that Massive were "three twats from Bristol" and most of the evidence points in that direction. Late nights at the Dugout, bombing the city's walls with graffiti, and the electric feel of a Wild Bunch sound system were all undoubtedly cool, expressions of a city with a clear sense of identity and place. But left to their own devices, Massive may have languished as one side project among many, a footnote in the annals of global hip-hop. Their synergistic connection with Cherry took them beyond the more stripped-down—and at times inchoate—sessions in Bristol and to the more slickly professionalized and globally integrated hub that was London, a place brimming with talent up and down the line, from stylists and photographers to string arrangers and studio engineers.

But the trappings of London do not come cheap, and in this sense, *Blue Lines* represents the passage from margin to center, underground to the mainstream, indie to major. Although budget figures are unavailable, a glance at the personnel and liner notes for the record evince a multilayered and skilled team working across multiple, storied locations. A Led Zeppelin project this was not, but Massive found themselves worlds away from the DIY channels of Bristol. The vinyl pressed up at the end of the day was emblazoned with "VG 50550"—a release by Virgin records.

Outside of Island or the legacy outfit EMI, Virgin was arguably the most recognizable British music label. It was somehow synonymous both with the scale and prestige of the majors and with a persistent countercultural credibility, associated with bringing radical sounds to a wide audience through its subsidiary imprints. Indeed, Virgin was founded by a group that included a then-twenty-three-year-old Richard Branson, and was emblematic of a 1970s Rock Establishment in which partying with the talent or smoking a joint in a meeting was not out of place. The label's young founder was equally at ease hanging out with Keith Richards as with signing self-immolating young acts like the Sex Pistols. By 1978, one imprint, Front Line, was churning out records by talent back in the Caribbean, bringing songs by legends like I-Roy and Gregory Isaacs to English shores. Of course, such savvy served the label well, and Branson went on to helm everything from record shops to hotels to aerospace companies under the Virgin banner.

And so, as the 1980s drew to a close and with the majors looking for the "next big thing," Bristol and its interwoven community of players and producers were firmly in the sights of Virgin. But who would be their breakthrough act? How to convince musicians from the underground—who shunned celebrity and had been doing it on their own, with total creative freedom—to take the plunge? Here the particulars get murky, but what is clear is that other Bristol groups had their chance and passed, and Massive themselves, then a studio spin-off from a more performance-based project, were not necessarily looking for major-label success and the attendant obligations and fanfare. In this sense, it seems, Cherry and her partner Cameron McVey were crucial—the one with her deep ties to the Bristol post-punk landscape and the other with his shrewd business sense and connections in the capital. They were both perfect intermediaries between these two worlds, and they were instrumental in shaping the tone and appearance of *Blue Lines* over the course of 1990.

Cherry, of course, had her own profile within the currents of popular hip-hop and R&B. She had a signature flow that was, by turns, assured or witty. Her sound was not only distinctive but also in sync with the sort of acts that were topping the American charts during the Spring of 1991, that is, Christopher Williams's "I'm Dreamin'" or Pebbles's "My Backyard."[1] But perhaps more importantly for Massive Attack, she was a kind of translator, someone who could find hidden gems below the mainstream radar and bring them to a wider audience. In one sense, she took Massive Attack out of obscurity, bringing them to London. In another sense, she owed them a great deal—the vitality and the immediacy of their UK-infused Wildstyle sensibility was baked into her breakthrough singles. "Buffalo Stance" boasts that Cherry is "lookin' good, hangin' with the Wild Bunch," even as the Wild Bunch itself was no more. The Nellee Hooper of 1988 was in London and working with another sound system that would become Soul II Soul. (Hooper went to produce for Madonna in 1994, on the Bjork-penned track "Bedtime Story," a trippy stand-out on an intentionally commercial record.) Meanwhile, Del Naja, Grant, and Vowles seem to have decamped, if temporarily, to the big city.

While much of the *Blue Lines* sound is down to the rich tones of the Coach House, other parts of the record were hashed out in a bedroom at Cherry's house in west London. Sections were recorded nearby at Eastcote Studios in

Ladbroke Grove, a neighborhood which was then a crucial hub in the west Indian music scene. If the Coach House exuded a kind of aura borne of technical wonkery and moody localism, Eastcote is far more pop establishment. It is now known for being the sort of place where the likes of Arctic Monkeys, La Roux, Paul Oakenfold, Mark Ronson, and, of course, Neneh Cherry have recorded. Eastcote is also a short walk to the Kensal Green tube station and the official mailing address of a production company called "The Cherry Bear Organization," listed as a contact address and producer of *Blue Lines*.

What to make of all these Buffalos and Bears? To understand that, and also why Cherry was so crucial to Massive, it helps to go back to the lead single for Cherry's 1989 breakout hit album *Raw Like Sushi*. Indeed, if someone were to revivify the 1980s from rogue DNA, like the fossilized mosquitos in Jurassic Park, they could do worse than start with "Buffalo Stance." It's fair to say the track would not have worked—or would have been far less compelling—without Cherry's exuberant, multiaccentual delivery, cheeky asides, and ironic self-awareness. But it's also fair to note that many of the key singles, like hers, that turned up on the UK dance imprint Circa Records were at once collaborative efforts and instances of deft cultural appropriation. In many ways, the song's lyrics amount to a roll-call of the wider social circle of the Cherry Bear group: one that included musicians, photographers, models, producers, and promoters, a group that had started to gel in 1987 under the aegis of designer Ray Petri, who envisioned the "Buffalo" ethos in the years leading up to his death in 1989.

The wider Buffalo collective included models such as Naomi Campbell, Tony Felix, and Talisa Soto, and budding commercial talent like Mark and James Lebon and Jean-Baptiste Mondino. The group was united by both a style and an ethos, one set on colliding seemingly disparate archetypes—high and low, the martial and the urban, masculine and feminine. If you remember the 1980s as a time where it was still acceptable to wear "African" sarongs and bite on Native American culture, then you have an inkling of what Buffalo was about. To Buffalo's credit, however, putting men in feminine-coded clothes looked forward to a mainstream more shaped by and accepting of queerness and queer aesthetics. Such openness to questions of gender, sexuality, and identity were all comparatively new in the 1980s, when Petri was soliciting stylish young urbanites to collaborate with him and build an iconic brand. On the flip side, it also raises some questions about cultural theft and uncritical appropriation—the very set of problems that would reemerge in debates around the ethics of sampling (think Moby's use of blues records on *Play* in 1999, or Enigma's controversial recording of an unknown Taiwanese Aboriginal singer).

Jamie Morgan, one of the Buffalo crew, recalled that Petri signaled the "birth of the stylist" (or in 2018 terms, the influencer, the lifestyle curator) as an industry job. But Buffalo also marked the beginning of closed circuit of "the street, the magazine, and the advertiser. Realizing that 'cool' can now be taken from youth culture and put into advertising. And now zzzzzip, it's a direct line."[2] Of course, packaging radical youth culture was by then a time-tested tradition, if not the direct pipeline that Morgan recalls (or the social media echo chamber of the present). As far back as 1939, the art critic Clement Greenberg argued that the avant-garde was always connected to the bourgeoisie by an umbilical cord of gold.

And closer to home, the impresario Malcolm Maclaren was already hard at work capitalizing on the fey stylings of London's "Blitz Kids" and the tattered graphic tees, leather fetish wear, and pyramid stud aesthetics of the first wave of punk. As of 1980, he had already established himself as a key purveyor and stylist of underground chic. What had been a small venture in the back of Chelsea's Paradise Garage became, in 1974, a store called Sex. He and his partner, former teacher/current Dame of the British Empire Vivienne Westwood, created a locus for the local cool kids, the ones who would go on to be leading lights in the gothic, punk, and Neoromantic subcultures that defined the early Thatcher years. Siouxsie Sioux shopped there, as did Adam Ant, and of course John Lydon of Public Image Ltd. He got his start at Sex too, when Maclaren brought together the four founding members of the Sex Pistols in 1975. After all, Andy Warhol had already proven with the Velvet Underground that having a good house band could do wonders for a brand.

By 1980, the Pistols were no more, but Julien Temple directed an arch postmortem called *The Great Rock'n'Roll Swindle*, which has Maclaren memorably discussing his formula for the band: make sure they can't play; make sure they hate each other. The eponymous song yelps, "'Cos we didn't give a toss/Filthy lucre ain't nothing new/But we all get cash from the chaos." In any case, the punk heroes of yore were already on to other things, new sounds to absorb emanating from the States. Maclaren assembled the group Bow Wow Wow from dissident members of Adam and the Ants. Their 1982 *Last of the Mohicans* record, with its faux-Manet cover and eclectic sartorial cues, presaged Petri's Buffalo sensibility. And that summer in 1980 saw The Clash visiting New York and channeling disco breaks and hip-hop patter into their "Magnificent Seven." The record was a key influence on a young Robert Del Naja.

All of which raises the question—was punk ever a transgressive force, or just a way to commodify dissent to make a quick buck at the expense of the rubes? Can a "collective" that cannibalizes the underground itself be "underground," a force of social disruption? Or is it just the last nail in the coffin, a cynical squeezing of the lemon before what was once a secret becomes a fad? Can fashion ever be a force for a radical social agenda, or is it all just good business, a great rock 'n' roll swindle? These are not questions I'm prepared to answer decisively, but these were important issues in the years after 1968, when folks wondered about the fate of the counterculture, about the energies of the avant-garde and leftist politics. In the 1980s, it was fair to wonder about how to resist in an age of Conservative resentment, cocaine-addled casino capitalism, and a backlash against people of color on both sides of the Atlantic.

Clearly, there are some parallels here: Maclaren's trotting out the Pistols as emissaries for his various enterprises echoes *Raw Like Sushi* and the records made within the wider Buffalo circle. Each was entangled in the marketing of youth culture in a complicated way. And it's a big enough question, about the social origins and later political outlook of Massive

Attack and those in their orbit, that the last chapter of the book deals with it head-on. For now, it is worth noting that Sex was a boutique dedicated to white rock 'n' roll, and the Pistols cheekily self-identified as "yobs"—a rude working-class lad.

But that was not the Buffalo—or the Massive—brand. As Cherry tells it, in the aftermath of Thatcher's election and the social disruptions of the late-1970s:

> Youth culture was intent on self-expression with a punk-DIY attitude. Life happened offline and in real time. There were no mobile phones, no internet. . . . Buffalo was an attitude and a way of living: it stands for rebellious self-expression, friendship, and a fearless creative spirit. It came together to support the work of genius stylist Ray Petri. The Buffalo crew were British, and mostly came from immigrant families and mixed up cultures.[3]

This "creative spirit" reaffirms the sense of collaboration and community at the heart of the Bristol music scene and UK bass culture more generally. These were scenes that refined an earlier avant-garde sensibility in which social mission takes precedence over celebrity or individual ambition. It's also important that, as Cherry notes, most of the people involved in Buffalo were what, writing at that exact moment, theorist Stuart Hall called "new ethnicities." These were the youth from the postcolonies and migrant neighborhoods that were redefining what it meant to be British, even as the country was roiled by racial tensions and xenophobic rhetoric.

Fair caveats, all, but the Maclaren connection doesn't end here. What was good for The Clash was good for the impresario, who was nothing if not an astute trendspotter. And in those years New York hip-hop was undoubtedly the "next big thing"—turntable scratches, funky Roland 303 bass lines, and shuffling, syncopated breakbeats. His own take, with the help of the Supreme Team, ended up becoming one of the iconic records of 1982, crystallizing the uptown sound and layering it with an infectious hoe-down hook: "Two Buffalo girls run 'round the outside, 'round the outside" The video, like Wild Style, is a visual encyclopedia of hip-hop culture, from breakdancing in Washington Square to the word Buffalo appearing in bright orange bubble letters. "Buffalo Gals" provides the iconic sample that cuts in between the verses of "Buffalo Stance," a scratched record making an echoed-out, percussive "chick chicka wahhhhh." It's pure 1980s gold, as is the squelchy synth that takes its ascending, arpeggiated run through the song's best moments.

That synth is a throwback to early 1980s New York and the afro-futuristic tones of Afrika Bambaataa, but also a then-contemporary nod to the psychedelic textures of Acid House. Acid was, by 1988, a dominant force in the British underground, thanks to the advent of MDMA and the emergence of clubs like the Hacienda in Manchester and Shoom in London.[4] Those acid sounds on Cherry's record would certainly have been influenced by one of the record's collaborators, the London-based producer Tim Simenon, who began recording as Bomb the Bass (a reference to aerosol bombing) around 1987. His records channeled the edgier tones of Chicago house and Detroit techno,[5] and his "Electro Ski" remix of "Buffalo Stance" was an instrumental banger ready for clubland. The single's record sleeve, predictably, featured a desaturated photo of Cherry amid a scrawl of gray lettering—what appears to a personalized graffiti tag.

But an earlier version of the song—a smoother, airier sketch really—appeared as a B-Side to the single "Looking Good Diving" by Morgan McVey. Aside from what would become the iconic acid synth line, her version "With the Wild Bunch" bears little resemblance to the original. It shouts out to the Bristol crew and more plainly borrows from the Maclaren track, adapted here as an anthem for her cohort of models and photographers. Of course, the McVey of Morgan McVey is Cameron, at the time a singer-slash-model. He had previously been part of the group BIM, which peaked in 1982 and made pretty great New Wave music, with four-on-the-floor beats and funky bass octaves. Cherry went on the marry McVey, and he reinvented himself as a manager and producer, going by the handle Booga Bear. And the Cherry Bear organization was born.

While there's good fun to be had laughing off old Morgan McVey videos on YouTube, it's also undeniable that McVey and the Buffalo crew were stone cold pros. By the time *Raw Like Sushi* was released in 1989, McVey had spent a decade in the trenches of the recording industry. As working models, he and Cherry had traveled widely and conformed to the protocols of a competitive, multibillion-dollar global industry that supported a gamut of other creative workers. If the Bristol archetype is one of anti-celebrity iconoclasm or a slightly narcotized, shambolic cool, the Londoners of Buffalo were a marked counterpoint. A promotional video from 1989 called "The Rise of Neneh Cherry" is a notable example. This major label-produced bonus video shows two things above all: that those managing Cherry's debut knew even before her record dropped that it might be useful to have live and behind-the-scenes footage on hand; and that her management team foresaw 1989 as a year when she would break through to the mainstream, not as an accident but as part of a multipronged, well-oiled rollout strategy.

It seems that much of this was down to McVey himself. There he is in the video—by now less glossy, more hip-hop impresario—in the room with Cherry and PR strategist "Tony the Greek," discussing the tactical benefit of releasing "Buffalo Stance" in the fall of 1988 and pairing it with saturated media coverage and touring to set up 1989 as the breakout year.[6] There he is again cutting in on interviews with reporters from the rock weeklies and large newspapers, monitoring the time, contact, exposure. And there's Cherry, performing again and again, on television, in clubs on the continent. On the evidence of the tape alone, whatever else Cherry Bear was, it was synonymous with conscientiousness and with media savvy. And while it's difficult to know what the factors are that put an act over the top and in to the mainstream while other talented peers languish, it never hurts to be connected with a group of industry professionals in the capitol, people who know the lay of the land and, in the case of Buffalo, know how to translate the underground into something more suited to mainstream tastes.

While neither Del Naja nor Cherry was willing to comment on the particular comings and goings in Kensal Green, there it is, on the liner notes—a call out to Cherry Bear. And it's likely no coincidence that *Blue Lines* was released on Circa Records in 1991, a dance imprint that released Cherry's singles, including "Buffalo" and "Kisses on the Wind" in 1988, *Sushi* in 1989, and the Cole Porter rework, "I've Got You Under My Skin" in 1990. Circa itself was a subsidiary of Virgin, which was on the lookout for emerging groups from Bristol to sign. But by all accounts, Cherry's own house was a base of operations—hanging out, recording, learning the ropes, even penning new music. For instance, "Hymn of the Big Wheel" was a collaboration with Cherry and Horace Andy. And while Del Naja, in designer mode, assembled the front cover for *Blue Lines*, the back—a simple photograph of the three principals crouched against a black backdrop—was shot by none other than Jean-Baptiste Mondino. The latter is a French-born photographer and video director who had already collaborated with Don Henley, Scritti Politti, David Bowie, Madonna, and, of course, his fellow Buffalo posse member, Neneh Cherry.

There were other photographs, too, inside the sleeve. These headshots were not Mondino's work, but Eddie Monsoon's. Another fashion (and, sometimes, fine art) photographer, Monsoon was already collaborating with Judy Blame—a punk-inspired stylist who emerged from the London Neoromantic scene and who worked in dialogue and in parallel with Ray Petri as part of the so-called "House of Beauty and Culture" group of designers that influenced an array of hipper, younger fashion magazines such as *i-D*. Blame himself is thanked by Massive for his visual direction on *Blue Lines*, and he would also work as a stylist for Cherry. Monsoon, in turn, went on to photograph Massive Attack throughout the ensuing decade. His show of photographs of Massive Attack, which opened in Tokyo in 2001, touted some fifteen years of projects with the group, suggesting that he, Buffalo, and the Wild Bunch had been in contact since as early as 1986.

It was a reciprocal arrangement then—Cherry Bear provided a multifaceted entrée to key players in the west London scene. They shared in the production, visuals, and recording of *Blue Lines*, and were even on the same label's roster for a time. But Massive brought something else to the equation. They were emissaries of a once-provincial coastal town that was, by the late 1980s, seen as the site of a new groundswell of gonzo talent—a generator of street style and new permutations of a transatlantic sound. Those who were plugged in to popular music the year of *Blue Lines*'s release might remember a parallel example, the release of Nirvana's *Nevermind* in September of 1991. While the Seattle-Bristol similarities have been dissected at length already, it's worth noting, too, that Nirvana had already been at work in a scene driven less by pop impulses than punk ones, but their crossover from Sub Pop to DGC, the move from Seattle to Santa Monica marked a jarring contrast in environment and expectation. It was widely reported that the very anxieties at the end of Kurt Cobain's life were those of "selling out," and of trying to make his way amid the slickness and the sunshine in the belly of the American recording industry. But he, too, was an emissary of a certain form of subcultural authenticity.

Massive Attack's own retreat from celebrity and publicity and their later turn toward more explicitly avant-garde forms of politics and performance offer peeks at a parallel world, what might have happened in the long run for Cobain. In the meantime, Massive, with Tricky and Horace Andy in tow, brought a jolt of the Bristol ethos into the Cherry Bear orbit. Cherry's 1989 single *Manchild* was produced by Bomb the Bass and Booga Bear, but it was cowritten by Del Naja. The A-Side is a smooth, string-laden R&B session that lays the blueprint for later jams in the genre by the likes of TLC. To wit, "Manchild" warns of the fleeting pleasure and enduring pain of dating a loser and the computer-assisted video seems like a warm-up for the classic TLC track "Waterfalls" (1995). The remix, by Massive Attack, takes "Manchild" into a different terrain altogether, distorting the cadences of the original. Cherry's voice is down in the mix in the Massive version, but it echoes and lingers between the syncopated percussion hits, which are the focal point here. The tone is druggier and dubbier, but somehow more propulsive. The record-scratched vocal and clipped samples of the orchestration, too, call ahead to Portishead's turntablist cinematics on 1994's *Dummy* (especially the song "Biscuit"). In style and tone, the remix also loosely adumbrates "Lately," one of Massive's songs with Shara Nelson.

Did Neneh Cherry and Cameron McVey "make" Massive Attack? It's difficult to say. How many things need to go just so for an album to land with its audience the right way, at the right time? What is the magic quotient, the sine qua non?

What is clear is that, in the years leading up to *Blue Lines*'s release—roughly 1988–1990—the boundary between Massive Attack and the Cherry Bear organization was porous, to say the least. They functioned together, these veterans of the Wild Bunch and the New Wave, of Bim and Bristol and Buffalo, and all the connective tissue between, as an extended form of collectivity. They inflected and impelled each other's efforts in an upward spiral to the mainstream. It would be an oversimplification to suggest that Massive were the cool ones while Cherry Bear and Buffalo were the connected ones—no, the subtlety and longevity of Cherry's and the Wild Bunch's cross-pollinations throughout the decade mean that the relationship was more complex than that. At the very minimum, the above should complicate the commonplace narrative that there was simply something in the water in Bristol and Massive Attack materialized, from the void, in the spring of 1991. *Blue Lines* was the result of a series of collisions and collaborations over several years— back at the Coach House, to be sure, but also in west London. It was a vital synergy, those twats from Bristol and their big-city cousins. Lookin' good, making hit records.

6
Flammable Materials

Did Banksy make the iconic cover of *Blue Lines*? Some people seem to think so. The logic here is a bit of the old "transitive property" from math class, so bear with me for a moment. You probably know about Banksy because he is the most famous street artist in the world. The Bristol-based painter's large-scale compositions on the sides of buildings, or his larger-scale interventions (on the partition wall in Israel, say, or in his "Dismaland" theme park) are the stuff of Pinterest fantasy and even the occasional theft of the very brick-and-mortar on which the work is realized. Banksy's work is smart, darkly humorous, and shot through with a political edge. It has long needled the police, military occupation, and the nationalist forces on the move in modern Europe. Based on his work, he seems like a cool guy.

While Banksy is, on the one hand, a canny self-promoter, unlike other street artists of his echelon—think Shepard Fairey—he has resisted the urge to unlock the bottomless reservoir of income to be had by licensing off his intellectual property to T-shirt makers and skateboard companies.

In short, Banksy is a massive international celebrity but retains his subcultural cred by carefully balancing exposure and overexposure, sincerity and cynicism, and (and this is crucial) by insisting on his anonymity.

Like Keyzer Soze, many people claim to know Banksy, or work on his behalf. He sometimes gives interviews and then denies having done so through a press agent. Banksy could be a design collective, a man or a woman, an old-school graffiti writer or an idle public school kid. Banksy's studious withholding has the effect of reinforcing an old punk rock dictum that runs from DC to Bristol: don't take the credit, don't be a celebrity . . . it's not about you. It also has the effect of stoking the mystery, fueling a sense that Banksy itself is a sort of meta-reflection on the nature of celebrity, access, and ownership in the global art world—an art world in which the United Kingdom has been a vital hub (especially in financing and the secondary market) for most of its recent history and, in particular, since the late 1980s.[1]

Banksy, for all of his internet and auction house–fueled celebrity, doesn't appear to be driven by personal fame or riches per se. He is claimed to have said, "I choose to keep my identity hidden because often when you know the artist, you think you also know the art and I want to keep the mystery. As well as that, the most noticeable and breathtaking pieces of street art are created by anonymous talents." According to the Western English magazine *Boundless*, he seeks to "concentrate on politics, culture, and society and give his take on war, poverty and how 'higher powers' can affect people."[2] Note the hedging in attribution here—these quotations are drawn from a Bristol publication that claims to have interviewed Banksy only to have a "Banksy representative" deny that the conversation took place. Now the important part: that interview was allegedly granted during the late summer of 2017 to clear the air, to declare once and for all that Banksy is not Robert Del Naja, also of Bristol.

Earlier that summer, a Twitter account went up purporting to be the "official" handle of Del Naja. It links out to the real Massive Attack page and includes, as of this writing, only four tweets. One read, "I confirm: I'm Banksy." The next, "I will never talk about Banksy, nor will I answer in his name." This is bizarre indeed, not least for the broken English throughout the page but also because it was directly contradicted in the months that followed by several purported Banksy interviews and, apparently by Del Naja himself onstage in Bristol. The uptick in interest was set off in June when the actor, DJ, and "yogangster" Goldie noted on the "Distraction Pieces" podcast that Banksy's name is Robert—a clue that was quickly cross-referenced with ongoing speculation including the multi-month investigation in 2016 by journalist Craig Williams who assiduously linked the appearance of Banksy pieces to cities where Massive played shows.[3]

Which is to say that trying to confirm whether or not Banksy and Del Naja are more than cross-town acquaintances is a bit of a pointless exercise. The work stands on its own, and exposing the one as the other adds little to one's understanding of that work. After all, Del Naja is notably wary of giving interviews, and he is himself a kind of anti-celebrity: the details of his life are not widely circulated but he can also be seen casually walking around town. Del Naja instead lets Massive's work speak for him, the project more significant than the man. This reticence became noticeably clear in the years after *Blue Lines* as the media firestorm of the mid-1990s began to recede, leaving a bitter taste for many artists and musicians in the West. (Of course, one might take Del Naja's very disposition as further grounds that he is indeed Banksy. And round and round it goes.)

For the purposes of this chapter, the Banksy story is important for one reason and one reason alone: it might answer the question with which we started. The Banksy claim is only plausible because Robert Del Naja is, indisputably, a very talented visual artist, and he designed the cover for *Blue Lines*. Beyond record sleeves, he is, unsurprisingly, a significant figure in the realm of street art, where he contributed to the formal evolution of the genre in two ways: by translating American aerosol culture into a British context, and by pioneering stencil-based compositions as a style that would radically shift the meaning of "graffiti" in the decades to come.

*****

The seminal 1983 film *Wildstyle* is one of the most important documents of both black diasporic counterculture and street art to ever be produced. To it, we should add two more watershed moments. The first is the publication of photographers Henry Chalfant and Martha Cooper's book *Subway Art* in 1984. In much the same way that the dramatized aerosol artists of *Wildstyle* made their way to high-visibility city walls and carefully guarded subway "layups," Chalfant and Cooper tracked this new form of painting as it circulated through the city on these whole car or whole train murals.

These rolling galleries carried the names of aspiring writers through the five boroughs, just as the *Subway Art* book, with its comprehensive scope and vibrant colors, functioned as a kind of viral document, a Rosetta Stone through which young artists the world over could learn the rudiments of a style of wild-style script, bubble letters, fluid arrows, humorous political commentary, and art historical citation that was actively negotiated during the "golden age" of the late 1970s and early 1980s in New York. If The Clash's "Magnificent Seven" and Ahearn's docudrama brought hip-hop to the Wild Bunch, then *Subway Art* touched off a global culture of tagging, throwies, and urban murals in the United Kingdom and beyond in what is now a canonical style. As Del Naja recalls, "We were all apprentices back then and hungry for new input and everything that came from NYC was absorbed and regurgitated. The *Subway Art* book became the graffiti artists' manual; we were all on the same page for awhile."[4]

The liner notes to *Blue Lines* makes these influences explicit, thanking Tats Cru, a Bronx-based aerosol collective (Brim, Bio, and Mack) who were foundational in generating the New York style of the early 1980s and who remain active muralists to this day. And sure enough, a photo in a recent compendium of Del Naja's visual art shows a scene from the Bronx, circa 1986. A youthful Goldie reclines with paint in hand alongside Tats Cru on the set of the film *Bombing* (the common term for clandestine painting), a documentary by Dick Fontaine for the recently launched BBC Channel 4. In fact, it was through the film—set in New York and Birmingham—that a denim-clad Del Naja meets the future drum & bass producer as they peruse the brutal sprawl of the local Council housing, enlivened only by Goldie's aerosol handiwork.

For his part, Del Naja was throwing up pieces—including the iconic tag that continued as his professional moniker, 3D—around Bristol, from the Stokes Croft neighborhood to the Caribbean enclave of St. Paul's. One might mistake these pieces for works by Dondi, Crash, or Lady Pink (straight from the outer boroughs) but for their local references: a "Wild Bunch" mural on Park Street, near the Dug Out and the University in central Bristol; 3D inscribed in drop block letters alongside a star and menacing "bobby," complete with elongated custodian helmet. Relations between the police and urban immigrant communities in the United Kingdom were particularly fraught throughout the first half of the 1980s, but 3D's mural points to themes common in New York graffiti as well—of police or city bureaucrats interfering with a new form of expression, arresting writers and sandblasting or "buffing" away fresh layers of spray paint. Another piece from 1984, in Stokes Croft, simply (if self-referentially) reads "It's No Great Crime."

But for most people at that time, graffiti was a "great crime," synonymous with a time in New York history when the city was on the verge of financial collapse—a case study in deindustrialization and urban blight. Yet the past several decades have seen the indisputable aesthetic and commercial breakthrough of street art, which draws tourists and social media interest from Stokes Croft to Shoreditch, Brooklyn to Berlin. In the mid-1980s, Del Naja remembers that the tagging revolution, a time when "everyone carried a fat marker" was underway, and more importantly, that "the criminal damage element . . . had soon overwhelmed the ambition of the art." By the 1990s, however—with the rise of Fairey, FAILE, Swoon, JR, and others—the dynamic had shifted. The work began taking on a more graphic than textual aesthetic, embracing techniques of stenciling and wheat paste pioneered in part by Del Naja. The "scene had completely changed," he recalls, "less hierarchy . . . and a lot more talent. It had evolved beyond its NYC roots. It was very international and become a serious commercial alternative to fine art."[5]

The visual aesthetic of Massive Attack, long central to its records and live shows, tracks with Del Naja's own evolution as a street artist. If the Wild Bunch started out as a Bristol variant on hip-hop culture, complete with wild-style murals, Massive has ended up in the rarefied air of serious contemporary art. *Blue Lines* itself was an important tipping point here, from its iconic paper sleeve to its interior graphics, to the series of small badges and icons that dot the periphery of the liner notes. The pictorial elements are Del Naja's, evidence of a shift around 1987 to a more studio-based practice that combined motifs from graphic design and gestural painting.

It makes sense, then, that there was another important touchstone in play here, also from New York. Jean-Michel Basquiat was something of a self-consciously high-brow version of the Wildstyle group. His work was never "Pop," but he sought out Andy Warhol and frequented the same East Village spaces in which uptown hip-hop and downtown art school folks rubbed shoulders after-hours. Once gallerist Anina Nosei got him painting actual canvasses in 1981, the sky was the limit. Del Naja saw Basquiat's work on a trip to

Japan in 1986, which profoundly impacted him. Basquiat "painted in a raw and confrontational way. He abused the canvas with chaotic composition and intense primary colors. . . . Basquiat inspired me to break away from the calligraphy of the traditional graffiti art form."[6] Certainly anyone who knows Del Naja's studio paintings, or stayed attuned to work on the covers of *Protection* and *Heligoland*, can see the influence of Basquiat's edgy, painterly handling of the human body.

But the *Blue Lines* era was notable for its decidedly graphic style. The materials for that album don't look like painting so much as graphic design of the sort you'd expect from glossy advertisements, magazines, or promotional materials. This is unsurprising, as bands have long relied on signature styles, badges, logos, and so on to crisscross the world on liner notes and patches and stickers. What's interesting here is that Massive did not outsource this work, but relied instead on a DIY ethos more suited to the post-punk and hardcore culture of the era, with its insistence on self-reliance and social critique.

Del Naja himself makes this fine line between art and branding—the self-awareness of which was a key part of the post-punk ethos—even blurrier. When asked about the cover art for *Blue Lines*, he notes that the "transformation of John Lydon from The Pistols to Public Image Ltd also had a big impact on me, musically and stylistically. Symbolically turning the band into a brand—a literal corporation—was a potent statement during Thatcher's Britain in the 1980s."[7] Thatcher, of course, had come to power in the 1979 elections with the help of advertising magnate Charles Saatchi who used clever slogans and billboards to help elect the Iron Lady. Her eleven-year leadership was, like Ronald Reagan's, synonymous with antagonism of unions, mishandling the AIDS crisis, dismantling the social safety net, and accelerating the free-market corporatization of the world. To "brand" oneself or one's band was to sardonically ape the dominant mores of the time.

And so, Massive's own iconic self-branding should also be understood in this light—an act of self-definition and also of layers of coded ambivalence. The record sleeve for *Blue Lines* introduced the world to the group's signature flame logo, seen spinning at the center of plates of black vinyl, on T-shirts, and tattooed on arms. It suggests an appropriation of both governmental and corporate signage, while also signaling the combustibility of the landscape of the 1980s, fueled by the twin engines of hip-hop and punk culture.

For Massive, two 1979 records proved pivotal in the design of their own. Public Image Ltd's *Metal Box* was issued with a novel kind of packaging—a metal tin cut to the size of the record, like an old-time film canister, and emblazoned with the PiL logo in the center. That same year, the Northern Irish band Stiff Little Fingers released its debut, *Inflammable Materials*, sporting a black sleeve, sleek sans-serif letters in red, and a grid of nine repeating small fires.

Massive paid tribute to PiL but went "downmarket," using cardboard rather than metal as a surface for screenprinting (a technique used by Warhol and for punk posters alike). At the center brown paper, the *Inflammable* logo appears anew, but returned to its source code: a black-bounded red diamond, reading FLAMMABLE 2. Widely available as signage and stickers, the *Blue Lines* flame is drawn from official UK and Commonwealth markers for the transit and storage of hazardous materials. Again, it was Del Naja who brought the design to the group. Already adept at flypasting and handling a scalpel, photographs document his piecing together the cover like a homemade 'zine. He had seen Stiff Little Fingers at Bristol's storied Colston Hall when he was 14. Their record design "always stood out . . . amongst all my punk records nothing was quite as graphic as that, as simple."[8]

And there was one final homage to *Inflammable Materials*: Del Naja appears to have borrowed the font from that record jacket as well. You might object that Stiff Little Fingers is written out in a thin, utilitarian ALL CAPS, where Massive is known for an iconic all lower case. Nonetheless, these are variants of the classic sans-serif Helvetica, designed in 1957 by Max Miedinger and one of the most celebrated fonts for advertising and graphic design of the late twentieth century. Massive's Helvetica is simply the bold oblique form of the familiar lettering. In its way, Del Naja's choice is a reference not only to that striking record in his crate but also to a wider adoption of European sans serifs in the 1980s by punk-inspired artists such as Barbara Kruger, Jenny Holzer, and the Guerrilla Girls, who used Futura in their graphically bold counterpropaganda. Theirs were art practices that sought to use the very language of advertising to subvert systems of social domination and, especially, the objectification of women's bodies. As historian Douglas Thomas has noted, "Futura is the lingua franca of 20th-century advertising. . . . So if you're trying to critique commercialism, what better than to use the same visual language as the advertisers themselves?"[9]

While Futura has a slightly more controversial history than Helvetica (one linked both to the Nazis and to the Apollo landing), it's fair to say that the use of bold mid-century fonts in general became associated with a style of appropriation, one aimed at using the corporatism of 1980s against itself. In this sense, the *Blue Lines* record bucked a then-contemporary trend of punk records using gothic, faux-stenciled, or hand-scripted type—see proximal releases by Depeche Mode and Sonic Youth, or Public Enemy and A Tribe Called Quest. Or indeed, as the 1990s began, a more disturbing trend began, with exaggerated, offbeat serif letters gracing the cover of bestsellers like Hammer's *Please Hammer Don't Hurt 'Em* and the eponymous *Marky Mark and the Funky Bunch*. *Blue Lines* exuded, by contrast, a restrained cool that gestured more toward the political avant-garde (and the likes of Jamie Reid and Banksy) than to earlier hip-hop signifiers or their contemporaries in mainstream pop music.

In retrospect, it's clear that monochromatic, lower-case Helvetica and its variants quickly became something of a calling card for the new UK scene that emerged alongside the young British artists and the rise of a post–Cold War Europe with London as its beating heart. Flipping through back issues of the pop weeklies, one starts to see adverts using what looks very much like Massive's signature lettering. Ironically, within a few years, a young band of Mancunians by the name of Oasis would use the same bold Helvetica in for their own white and black logo. It would be stamped prominently on the cover of their blockbuster 1994 record *Definitely Maybe*, a cornerstone of a new Britpop and of the so-called second British Invasion.

7
Daydreaming

In 2001, Michael Winterbottom released a film called *24 Hour Party People*, which chronicles the rise of the "Madchester" boom that gave the world the British rave scene, the Ibiza cliché, and the swaggering, jangly Britpop of the 1990s. There is plenty of good work on this topic, including the memories of people like Peter Hook—the bassist for Joy Division and New Order—who were on the ground during those crucial years of the mid–late 1980s, years when scads of young Brits turned on the MDMA and flocked to disused industrial spaces in the city. The film itself centers on the TV personality turned Factory-records exec Tony Wilson, and essentially tells the biopic tale of Joy Division and post-punk on the one hand, and the Happy Mondays and the emergence of Acid House on the other.

At its best, though, *24 Hour Party People* makes some compelling arguments about how music itself was changing in the 1980s. In one scene at Wilson's mega-club the Hacienda, one of the Factory cohort wonders aloud about the DJ booth, asking who is going to pay to watch a person simply play records from an elevated perch in the club. This is a fair point, the 1980s after all being a high water mark for a certain kind of media-exposed musical celebrity—an era of epic bands like U2 or Aerosmith, bards like Bruce Springsteen or Kate Bush, and bloated concept records produced in the wake of Pink Floyd and the prog rock of the 1970s. Think back to the clarion call of "Death to Disco"; recall that, throughout the decade, dance music had largely been driven back underground. The last time most folks had thought about disco, it still had an analog glow about it, animated by feminine vocals à la Debbie Harry or Donna Summer.

The Happy Mondays embodied this tension: if New Order was the financial lifeline for the Hacienda, the Mondays were something of a house band, and their approach blended elements of Acid, psychedelic rock, and disco. They made propulsive songs with a multicultural vibe, nonetheless overlaid with prototypical British whiteness (here channeled by the inveterate libertines that were the Ryder brothers—in retrospect, a kind of Noel and Liam Gallagher v. 1.0). This formula allowed young audiences to have their cake and eat it too, listening to laddish pub music built on a foundation of black American styles, notably the funkier sounds coming out of places like Chicago and New York.

Of course, remixers of Mondays records, like Paul Oakenfold, were "turned on," so to speak, at those Mancunian and Balearic parties and gave the world, you know, trance. In Simon Reynolds's estimation, a great deal of 1990s-era electronic music denuded all that was transgressive of American house music—its blackness, its soul, its sexiness—and made it sterile, posthuman. The Mondays marked a middle point on this journey, from disco to trance and progressive house. They retained the glitchiness and unpredictability of the human element, but their best moments were essentially forerunners to those of their peers in the years that followed: 4/4 beats, looped piano lines, and soaring diva vocals. In one particularly stirring moment from Winterbottom's film, a shot moves from an aerial view of the Hacienda, and then takes the viewer into its Dionysian, kaleidoscopic interior. A fragment of the Mondays' "Hallelujah" plays, with its chiming piano sample cranked beyond 100 BPM, and Kirsty MacColl shouting "higher" to rafters in disco-operatic tones. It's futuristic and angelic at the same time, laying the blueprint for the underground deep house or commercial forays like Moby's 1995 *Everything is Wrong*. This is the moment, the Tony Wilson character reminds us, when the Hacienda became a new cathedral. This is where the DJ was anointed, the beat beatified.

And the above is also the exact cultural landscape in which Massive Attack was formed, one in which the underground was being cultivated for the mainstream, and in which bands were slowly giving way to production teams—but not quite yet. In the antediluvian world before the internet and Spotify, before Diplo and Calvin Harris, audiences still wanted a band, recognizable people who they could see on a stage or hang pictures of on bedroom walls. To buy a record was a deeply personal choice, an investment and signifier of identity. It's no surprise, in fact, that that the indie and college rock that effloresced in the 1990s tended to undermine the grandiosity of the 1980s pop star with studied irony and sarcasm. Massive shared these impulses—the same anti-celebrity ethos, the same collectivist tendencies, the same western England reserve that made the work of peers like Sonic Youth a post-post-punk exercise in purification. But Massive, too, were rooted in a more human-scale style of performance, in the sociality and collaboration of the Wild Bunch sound system, before they became, in effect, studio musicians, producers. And then, there was the issue of selling records.

As journalist Michael Gonzalez recalls, even when he interviewed Massive on the eve of the release of *Mezzanine* in 1998, "the group itself was still somewhat anonymous. They could walk around the city without being bothered." They weren't immediately identifiable, snap-shot-ready celebrities, even if they had released, already, two of the most definitive records of the decade and were on the way to a third. This is partially because they had spent much of the previous fifteen years not playing instruments at all. As Grant Marshall (Daddy G) remembers,

> In the beginning, the sampler was our main musical instrument . . . when we first formed Massive Attack, basically we were DJs who went into the studio with our favorite records and created tracks. At the time, we tried to rip off the entire style of American hip-hop performers, but we realized, as artists, it's important to be yourself. We realized it made no sense for us to talk about the South Bronx. Slowly but surely, we had to reclaim our identities as Brit artists who wanted to do something different with our music.[1]

In this transition, Massive already had three aces in the hole. One, of course, was Tricky himself, who exuded an off-kilter charisma and traded memorable verses with Del Naja in his inimitable Knowle West drawl. The other two were Shara Nelson and Baillie Walsh. Nelson was the diva, and Walsh the filmmaker who brought both Tricky and Nelson into the limelight, making them the faces of Massive Attack in a series of four videos for *Blue Lines*. For her part, Nelson was already an established singer, releasing a series of singles starting in 1983. By 1990, her position with Massive was loosely defined. More than a session musician, she collaborated on at least five tracks with the group, including the outtake "Just a Matter of Time," which was released as a stand-alone video. The song is a bit of trippy marginalia, with its Smith & Mighty-style breakbeat, and fugue-like vocal fragments looping and washing over each other low in the mix. The video is a mini-surrealist film, reminiscent of something Maya Deren or Luis Bunuel might have dreamed up fifty years earlier. The unifying force here is Nelson's expressionistic improvisation, and her lucid voice floats through a field of workaday samples and conversational snippets.

Nelson didn't continue with the group after *Blue Lines*, however, noting that "it's a pity how things ended up with me and Massive Attack. Put simply, the structure of the band changed, and we didn't get the same vibe working together. But I'm still hugely proud of the album we did together." In some ways, this is unsurprising. Massive's lineup was in flux consistently through the end of the 1990s, and many of their most celebrated singles are collaborations with talented women. One need look no further than 1998's "Group Four" and "Teardrop," which both relied on the diaphanous soprano of Scottish singer Liz Frazer, formerly of the Cocteau Twins.

And, of course, the all-time-classic "Protection" from the album of the same name is a fluid synthesis of Massive's spare production and the mournful torch singing of Everything But the Girl's Tracey Thorn, who penned the lyrics in absentia after being sent a demo tape in the mail.

An epistolary collaboration with Thorn was, in fact, altogether part of the Massive's MO. In a review for the reissued *Blue Lines* in 2012, a critic for the *Guardian* notes that, early on, "Massive Attack were not a pop group per se. Like Soul II Soul and various constantly fluid rap outfits, they were a collective who did not play any instruments themselves and employed other artists to augment—and in some cases—define their electronically driven sound and vision."[2] This was certainly true of the *Blue Lines* sessions, which Del Naja described as animated by a sense of chance and openness. For instance, looking back to the autumn of 1990, the string arranger Wil Malone says, "As I remember it, the band weren't even at Abbey Road when we did the strings! They seemed to be a very loose collective in those days. From my point of view, the producer Jonny Dollar seemed to be in charge."[3]

One of Nelson's key contributions was in August of that year back in Bristol, as the group were teasing out the songs that would make the final record. In her recollection, they were struggling to lay down a song called "It Will Rain," to no avail. She took a break to collect her thoughts and started to sing a vocal phrase that caught the ear of Dollar and Andy Vowles—the one started to play synth strings and the other tapped out a provisional beat.

The next month, a veritable wall of sound was being orchestrated in one of the most famed studios in the world, ready to be fused with drums from a reworked Paul Simon tune, "Take Me to the Mardi Gras." Like many of the songs from this period, "Unfinished Sympathy" was a collective effort, by a group of young artists playing influences and momentary inspirations off each other. It would take several months to be realized, but the heart of the song was conceived in an afternoon and rooted in Nelson's simple "I know that I've imagined love before." In the final version, Nelson takes these words from the tones of rueful observation to gospel sublimity. Many critics, musicians, and casual listeners consider "Unfinished Sympathy" to be the most beautiful "dance" record ever produced. It was the first single from *Blue Lines*, released two months in advance of the album in February of 1991, and was most people's first introduction to Massive Attack.

In this sense, one could be forgiven for thinking of Nelson as an integral member of the group, as her voice appeared on something like half the record. In early promotional photographs like an April 1991 cover of *Melody Maker* announcing "Massive: Heading for the Big Time"—there she stands with Del Naja, Marshall, and Vowles looking like a boss frontwoman. Shara Nelson was the first face of Massive Attack, the camera following her as she walks Los Angeles's Pico Boulevard in their breakthrough video for "Unfinished Sympathy."

That video was the second to be released, after the single-scene set piece that was "Daydreaming." While

"Daydreaming" provided a clear window into the group's personal idiosyncrasies and stylistic influences (Del Naja's rasta crown is impressive here; Tricky peers through a microscope while Marshall has his fortune read), it was, nonetheless, conventional. It relied on the nonsensical lip-syncing that pervaded even the most daring videos of the era. But for director Baillie Walsh, there was another problem. "Daydreaming" portrayed Massive as a band from a sleepy little town, rather than as the bleeding edge cosmopolitans that they were. "I really felt the international vibe in their music," Walsh recalls. "It had so many references to American music, to hip-hop, to all of those other places. And I didn't want them to be portrayed [as a small collective from Bristol], because their music is so much bigger than that."[4] For "Unfinished Sympathy," Walsh wanted a different approach.

Massive had been connected with Walsh the previous year through the stylist Judy Blame who, at the time, was working as a creative director of sorts for the group. Blame was impressed by Walsh's work for the Culture Club's Boy George. "Generations of Love" was only the second video Walsh had made at the time, but it was already a pioneering instance of the genre, by turns risqué and formally novel. Simply put, it is a gritty pseudo-documentary of the flesh trade in London, all working girls in SoHo's smut district picking up pallid, crustified johns and trading blow jobs for cash in a seedy theater. As an inspired meta-easter egg, Walsh—himself a former dancer—produced a stylish porno film, the one glittering on the screen in the too-well-lighted movie house. And the celebrity musician who wrote "Generations of Love"? No miming the words for Boy George—he only appears in the side of the frame, elegant in eyeshadow and brimmed hat, looking on at the antics in his midst.

"Generations of Love" was precisely the sort of video that marked, in those pre-YouTube days, differences in European and American cultural sensibilities. Circa 1990, it was quite likely that such an explicit video would only appear on MTV or VH1 after-hours, if at all—by no means a surefire strategy for launching a pop career. But Walsh's daring is precisely what made him a good fit for Massive, and their collaboration set up a long-standing ethos for the group, to produce artistically memorable projects rather than palatable ones. According to him, Massive

> wanted me to take risks. I felt very much because they loved 'Generations of Love,' which is very risky and never got played anywhere . . . they liked that risk-taking. They liked that it wasn't playing to MTV or playing to anywhere in particular. They wanted to find an audience that would find them. If it wasn't going to be broadcast, people would find it, somehow.

Walsh recalls the looseness, the collaborative spirit that suffused his time with the group. The success of "Daydreaming" begat the video for "Unfinished Sympathy" which explored a much wider terrain than their first outing: shot in full color, the group is not present save for Nelson, who walks down a bustling California street, lost in her thoughts. There is a more plainly narrative quality here, the sorrow of the lyrics reflected in Nelson's wistful expression and the distractedness of her progress through the city. True to Walsh's aim, there's no sense of Britishness as such here but, instead, a more universal story. That story is told through a technically difficult tracking shot that had to be carefully staged and blocked out in advance, all parts firing in sequence. He recalls,

> I see Shara walking in this hypnotized state, trance-like state, walking down the street, and it's one take . . . in the storytelling, that's me. When you're walking down the street when you've been hurt, you're in a trance—I don't notice anything that's going on around me. I've got from A to B and I haven't noticed anything on that journey, right?

The final product looks effortless, but the shoot was marked with difficulty, from the precise sequencing to the physically exhausting task of tracking Nelson's movement with the Steadicam. The latter proved so demanding that the plan to move the camera up to a crane and to a dramatic wide shot of downtown LA had to be abandoned. Massive and Walsh were disappointed that the original plan did not come to fruition, making the video's release bittersweet. "Unfinished Sympathy" did, however, go on to become a major success, one of the most widely discussed "electronic" singles of the decade and a landmark production at a time when music videos were increasingly seen as opportunities for young cinematic talent to make meaningful short-form work. The blockbuster videos of that year—like REM's "Losing My Religion," Michael Jackson's "Black or White," Red Hot Chili Peppers's "Give it Away," even UK #1 Bryan Adams's "Everything I Do"—experimented with evocative visuals (REM), iconic/bizarro performance (Chili Peppers), or purloined sequences from actual movies (Adams). But few cut the band out altogether, and fewer still, if any, so radiantly captured quiet human textures the way Walsh did. Like Massive's music more generally, the typical melodrama and loud spectacle of the video format were sidestepped in favor of something more measured, more sophisticated.

Massive and Walsh collaborated on two more videos in 1991. For "Safe from Harm," the group returned to London on the logic that they had already demonstrated the more global scope of their interests and ambitions. This video, too, relies on dynamic cinematic movements, panning high and low, following Nelson again—this time as she makes her way up the stairwell of a Council Estate. Readers who followed the Grenfell fire tragedy of June 2017 know the type, a looming tower of tight corridors, here populated by shadowy figures. The camera tracks past Del Naja, who grins devilishly and wags his finger in a gesture of warning; and then Vowles, leaning implacably in a door frame, and a boy wearing Freddy Kruger regalia. For this shoot, an abandoned tower in east London was scouted, and Walsh brought in the late scenic designer Alan MacDonald to build out the set—adding bits of furniture, heightening the scrawls of graffiti, installing ominous, flickering lights. In the end, the video exudes a feeling of claustrophobia and foreboding, with Del Naja racing up the lift as Nelson tries to reach her door. Walsh notes that the inspiration was an actual visit to a friend, Leigh Bowery (the art director for "Unfinished Sympathy"), where he "noticed I was really uneasy when I got to the tower block, and there were gangs of kids around . . . going into the stinking stairwell. It was spooky. And I just, and I thought, there you go . . . traveling up and up and up in a spooky tower block." A horror film in miniature, "Safe from Harm" concisely communicates the sense of anxiety felt by women in everyday life, and by working people living in mean conditions.

Walsh and Massive came full circle with the video for "Be Thankful for What You've Got," a slow burning soul cover, less obvious as a single but more or less perfect to set the stage for a short film, especially one suffused with the sort of low-key, louche energy of the result. A bare lightbulb with a fly buzzing distractingly about tracks down to a young woman singing to herself, the familiar bars of "Safe from Harm." She too is "living in her headphones," gathering a last moment of privacy amid some blaring background music as she clocks in for a shift. For a full ninety seconds, Walsh takes us through the back stage—makeup table, costume rooms, casual banter about the crowd—as the woman is transformed. We follow a figure in a blond wig draped in a pink boa as she makes her way up a prop elevator and, finally, into the theater. It's not Shara Nelson but, indeed, the stage show at a SoHo gentleman's club—the Ritz, complete with vaudeville lights and soaring flutes. It's all fittingly late 1970s vintage. Our dancer vamps to a more lushly orchestrated mix of the Massive track, seductively stripteasing to the beat, first to black lingerie, and finally, fully nude, save for the boa. No band, no diva, just a lady at work in central London.

"Be Thankful" was set at a real club, the Raymond Review Bar. Walsh recalls that the "stripper video was something I always wanted to do, because . . . I used to strip there, and I used to dance there. I always thought this would be an amazing place to make a little film." In the years before internet porn, to see a fully nude revue was rare. Far from the anonymity of a laptop in the bedroom, one had to venture out to a subsection of strip clubs, or the spicier racks of the print-magazine trade. In those days, it took real commitment. And here was a still relatively unknown group and a young director, fusing the subcultural day-to-day of London with the sanitized, broadcast-friendly currents of MTV. Suffice to say, the video got little rotation—again, a counterintuitive move for a band on the make. But according to Walsh, "it was the last video, and it just seemed really right and appropriate. [Massive] didn't really mind that there wasn't a way, that it wasn't going to be broadcast at midday on MTV."

In this sense, "Be Thankful" was a turning point. If the first videos from *Blue Lines* hewed to the conventions of the lip-syncing lyricist, the last installment pivoted to a form of anonymity, one that prized creativity and collaboration over celebrity. The work to follow continued on this trajectory. "Karmacoma," from the *Protection* record, was classic Brit-Pop in its hyper-saturated colors and Euro-hotel peregrinations. But like "Be Thankful," the song is submerged in the mix, like an underground river . . . just a sonic texture beneath hushed dialog. There are clear callouts to *The Shining*, and it looks ahead to the new generation of British gangster films that would typify the late 1990s. This is the terrain where Massive would ultimately make their mark—a murky turn-of-the-millennium landscape in which lush, if nocturnal, emanations from the UK were sui generis.

It is also clear that once on the far side of *Blue Lines*, Massive became increasingly media shy, more interested in letting the work speak for itself. As we will see, that work increasingly included taking clear political positions, and relying on collaboration as a primary medium. A striking example of this was the 2013 performance *You Are the Center of Everything* with British artist Adam Curtis. The show used archival film and sonic composition to draw together hidden connections—between neoliberal capitalism and foreign policy in the Middle East, or with Massive, the hidden vectors of the mid-century modernist juggernaut that still define our daily lives. Part scored film, part concert, part installation, it was a multisensory bonanza that defied easy categorization. An extended Massive lineup provided that sound, but the figures were near unrecognizable, hidden behind scrims of fabric, amplifying the ominous, immersive quality of the piece. Again, the focus was on ideas, on sensation, not on the people behind the boards.

This sensibility is on display in the early Baillie Walsh videos too, as Massive went from an unruly collective with a charismatic front woman (Nelson) to a more tightly defined project—one beginning to isolate its cinematic sweep and auteurist ambitions. They came of age alongside the Glazers and Trent Reznors and Johnny Greenwoods of the world, all of whom made the leap from the confines of 1990s rock to world-class virtuosity across a range of formats. Marshall remembers that "Baillie really did have a take on Massive Attack, he really did his homework about us—he started making videos around the same time we started making music so it was kind of this adventurous venture, it was exciting."[5] With Walsh's help, and in contrast to their peers,

Massive captured the overlooked byways of life in the British city with a blend of insouciant flair and quiet mysticism. Watching the countdown of the top 100 videos of 1991, there was simply nothing like it. Massive promised a world to come as a new generation claimed the means of production.

8
Big Wheel Keeps on Turning

Around the time that *Blue Lines* was reissued in 2012, *Rolling Stone* released a list of the 500 most important records of all time. Sure enough, Massive's debut made the cut, clocking in at 397. The short review points out that it is the first "post-hip-hop classic," gave birth to what "used to be called trip hop," and was "one of the most influential albums of the Nineties."[1] And as the *Pitchfork* reviewer from the same year put it, to listen to *Blue Lines* is "like reading an old William Gibson novel that describes the then-near future, which is now the present, with unsettling precision."[2]

One wonders, then, which future the reviewer had in mind. How, indeed, was *Blue Lines* influential? Did it presage a world in which breakbeats and electronic production undergirded virtually all pop music? Did it burst through the very sorts of genre distinctions, the boundaries between high and low, old and new classics that glossies like *Rolling Stone* so carefully enforced? Did it end the era of guitar rock once and for all, pointing the way toward a truly post-hip-hop (i.e., post-analog, post-instrumental) world?

Nothing so grandiose, I think. Though elements of each of these questions get at something true. On a slightly smaller scale—and based on purely nonscientific and anecdotal information—I gather that *Blue Lines* still gets credit (or maybe blame) for two trajectories.

One is that Massive laid out a blueprint for studio-based productions meant for listening at a relaxed pace, preferably at night, possibly with some mind-altering substances close by. On the one hand, *Blue Lines* was inward looking, insofar as it made music that was too slow for dancing, too subtly modulated for raging, but too dynamic for sleeping. Grantley Marshall was still DJing when *Blue Lines* came out, and he remembers that there "was a sense that there was something different that we were creating. . . . You've come home and you're off your head and you want to relax, let your head do the dancing rather than your feet."[3] Records like this reward careful listening, but can just as easily fade into the background. On the other hand, *Blue Lines* is also outward looking, deftly incorporating samples, callouts, and stylistic influences that cross-cut many decades and several continents. As original as it was on its release, it opened the floodgates to contemporaries who made music that was at once solipsistic and worldy, savvier than easy listening or acid jazz, but smoother than the currents of rock or hip-hop, especially in the grunge and gangster-dominated years of the early-1990s.

In this sense, it was easy to lump Massive in with their moody contemporaries Morcheeba, Nightmares on Wax, UNKLE, and, later, crossover acts like Zero Seven or Thievery Corporation. The success of those groups and the rise of corporatized yoga and wellness culture begat an entire cottage industry of "global chill" and "kundalini grooves"-type subgenres, populated by a steady stream of faceless producers working from laptops. And you'll probably rediscover many of the above groups yourself, while idly flipping through a range of anodyne Apple Music playlists. Not that there's necessarily anything wrong with that—it's all well and good to age out of childish things, and to move through adult life to tunes with just enough edge to feel like you haven't sold out your bohemian roots. Certainly, Massive invited this sort of comparison with songs such as *Blue Lines*'s closing number, "Hymn of the Big Wheel." It features Horace Andy once again, gently intoning lyrics like "the ghetto sun will nurture life / And mend my soul sometime again / The big wheel keeps on turning / On a simple line day by day / The earth spins on its axis / One man struggle while another relaxes."

There's something meta going on here—allusions to the broad tapestry of existence, the possibility of reversal and change. Andy paints a portrait of the complexities of the urban grind, nay the human condition, the water cycle, photosynthesis, the rotational velocity of the planet. Maybe the big wheel *is life*, man. More likely it's samsara, the always churning cycle of illusion, birth, suffering, and death. This makes sense for a group that cited Mahavishnu Orchestra as a key influence, looking unrepentantly back to the 1970s and the new-age holdvers of the era. Plus, Massive came together in the midst of one of the largest Hindu populations in the world, and in the immediate shadow of Rasta culture with its intimations of hidden worlds and a lost Zion. Of course, add a dash of samba, and you're most of the way to Thievery Corporation's easy-going pastiche. Yet, Massive's version of things was first marked by a certain optimism rather than the calculated naiveté/cynicism of the music piped in to the local Lululemon. That optimism was chipped away as the years wore on, as *Mezzanine* and what followed provided much darker, much tougher fare. But by 1998, of course, the damage was arguably done.

Conversely, it's easy to look back on *Blue Lines* as the beginnings of a truly British form of urban music, one that spoke to the specific contours of black life in England. In this account, the very toughness that unfolded in Massive's career was inevitable, and their early mutations of breakbeats and rapping opened the door not only to Tricky's own brand of psychedelic horror-core but also to the "grime wave" that began to crest in the mid-aughts, typified by MCs such as Dizzee Rascal and Wylie—both artists who are unabashedly black and British. In this way, grime and its relative subgenres meant something altogether new, but prefigured by Robert Del Naja listening to "Radio Clash" and watching Futura 2000 tag the walls of New York, thinking that maybe that source code could be imported, grafted into a new host.

For all that, even a cursory listen to these more recent British hip-hop records suggests a different lineage—with their sped-up beats and thickly accented raggas, the Wileys of the world seem to emerge from a different branch of the family tree, albeit one that runs right through Bristol, the Dugout, and the social scene around the Wild Bunch, Smith & Mighty, et al. Indeed, at the same time Massive Attack was coming together in London, a new sensibility was abrew, growing out of dancehall culture and the explosion into the market of new synthesizer technology. Someone should write that history, which centers on another group of Bristolians: Fresh 4 and, later, Reprazent. The breakbeat records that they produced concurrently with *Blue Lines* and *Protection* defined a new current of drum'n'bass and black diasporic music for decades to come. One could scarcely escape the 1990s without hearing some version of Roni Size's "Brown Paper Bag." These players ran in the same Bristol circles, cited similar source material, but were nonetheless on a parallel track to Massive.

Comparisons and citations aside, I think that, in the end, it is a fool's errand to try to classify Massive Attack's music, then as now. As Del Naja points out:

> Our history comes through all of these scenes when we've been about which were really effective for us. Hip-hop was a mirror of the punk movement, a new identity of something that was antiestablishment, of something that was independent from the mainstream. But when it came to putting our music about, we never felt like it really fit into any of the footprints anyone else were sort of treading—it's not what the DJs wanted to put on, and we weren't the darlings of the indie rock press either. We sort of trickled into the gaps. People had to find us in a different way.[4]

Even in 2010, with the release of *Heligoland*, Del Naja and Marshall still contended that they were comparative outsiders, and that from the outset, what they were up to went against the grain of the established musical order, certainly with respect to mainstream radio or the press. Marshall observed that year that "we've gone fifteen years now and we haven't really cut any turf in America. They don't really understand it . . . the black guy, the white guy, the mixed-race guy. It was like, how the fuck do you market this?"

I contend that among this studied ambiguity, *Blue Lines* was not just influential, but politically vital, in two related ways. The first has to do with to the emergence of Tricky, and Roni Size, and Goldie, and Wiley, and of bass culture more broadly. The connection is this: during the 1980s there was a culture war underway in England and the global North more broadly. The stakes were no less than who counted, who got to be "us," and who was relegated as "them." "We" got to be Western, affluent, respectable. "They" were demonized as aliens, given substandard housing, put at risk of deportation or harassment by the police. This battle was being played out in the streets, of course, and on TV news or in the rhetoric of Parliament. And this battle was staged in record stores, at the club, and in warehouses and parks during the gloaming of the twentieth century. In this culture war, popular music made a difference.

Records like *Blue Lines* therefore did important work precisely because they incorporated styles drawn from Britain's anti-Conservative punks and black immigrants, and because they carried all of these worlds in the same breath. *Blue Lines* was significant because it posited the opposite of "Little Britain." Like the Buffalo crew before them, they charted another course, one in which a black guy, a white guy, a mixed-race guy could all make music with soul singers and electronic producers and torch singers and roots-reggae legends. And *that* could be the future. As Del Naja himself says, "*Blue Lines* reflected a period in time we'd come from in Britain. It was less of a political statement and more of an image of the social environment—of Bristol, of London, of England, of the sort of characters and people that made up that landscape."

And so, the second crucial point has to do with Massive's timing. As the Berlin Wall came down and Conservatism seemed to recede, as the boom years of the 1990s unfolded in much of the world, the future seemed open for the first time in decades. One response to this new horizon was, as Massive are quick to point out, a kind of self-centeredness ranging from Gen-X jadedness and irony to the waves of technicolor frivolity surging across pop culture. This was, after all, the era of "New Labour" and Bill Clinton and, with them, the sitcom *Friends* and the return of feel-good guitar rock, be it Matchbox 20 or Spacehog or the Verve. The sharper edges of 1980s subculture seemed, for many, to have been sanded away. Others, however, were optimistic: the critic Mark Fisher believed that the music of a younger generation, exemplified by Goldie and Tricky and Massive, symbolized a new social trajectory, one that was from the outset "contaminated" by otherness.

Fisher thought underground music in the 1990s was mutating in ways that might light the way to a more inclusive (and interesting) version of modern life.[5] This, it seems, is the real connection between the radical musics of the 1990s— not "influence" or proximity but a shared resistance against white monoculture. This dimension of Massive makes it no surprise that even as they were looked over by the hip-hop establishment, they were also not the "darlings of the rock press." It's why, frankly, *Blue Lines* is so far down on that *Rolling Stone* top 500 list. Because that list is topped by not one, but three Beatles records; a top five still living in the conservative, lily-white 1960s that Oasis and their imitators so feverishly sought to mimic. Massive and their records were by contrast staged implicitly and explicitly against that past and its revivalists. They looked instead into an ambiguous future without boundaries, and of their own invention.

Of course, that future came about in many ways, but not in the utopian spirit once imagined. Quite the opposite—those dragged into a cosmopolitan world against their will have not gone quietly. And as recent years have made clear, history is doomed to repeat itself. Del Naja recalled in a recent radio interview that, they "started [*Blue Lines*] in a Conservative government in Britain after a long period of Thatcherism as we called it . . . we had the optimistic moment when the Labour Party came to power and then that went tits up when they went into Iraq and the recession that followed it."[6]

For Mark Fisher, these failures consign us to what he calls "hauntology." That is, our collective fate to live in the shadow of a life that could have been, but did not materialize. One symptom, concurrent with Massive's first few records, was the turning away from politics in a great deal of hip-hop and rock music. Another was the staging of the British mainstream not as cosmopolitan, but the opposite: the narcotized lack of affect in electronic music[7] or lost weekends at the Cafe del Mar on the one hand, and the embrace of Manchester cock-rock nostalgia on the other. By the end of 1990s, the chief musical exports from England were Ibiza trance compilations and swaggering rock 'n' roll records—easily digestible music for the punters who wanted little more than to let the good times roll.

But during those years, Massive Attack provided a bulwark against white mediocrity, against fratboy chauvinism or City of London greed. *Blue Lines* was a note from underground, an emblem of the anti-Thatcher and multicultural voices that constitute life as it is actually lived in English cities. It owed its existence to the unique environment of 1980s Bristol, but it also spoke to a larger mosaic of Britishness, alluded to a more global and humanistic agenda. From there, Vowles, Marshall, and Del Naja (to say nothing of Horace Andy, Tricky, and the rest) continued to rip up their blueprint, to keep things strange, alluring, haunting, and unsettling. That remains the most important legacy of the record and that which followed—that it asked us to get comfortable with the spaces between things, to keep our receptors open to new possibilities.

Massive explained it back in April of 1991 when the record hit the shelves. The pages of the *NME* were awash with more of the same, as the music industry churned out insipid Brit pop while Iraq burned. It's important to remember that the first thing Massive did with their newfound fame was to call out the war, call out corporate profiteering, dropping the "Attack" from their name. They've scarcely relented since. And what should have been an anodyne press tour often devolved into headier stuff, about openness to inspiration, and to new pathways into the world. The last word, then, goes to Del Naja, speaking to a reporter as their first record began its improbable ascent: "That's what *Blue Lines* is all about—the blank space that goes on forever, and people's fear of it. As soon as you let your defenses drop there's that blank space waiting for you, and that's why people go mad. Because if you don't carry on thinking about life everyday, the *Blue Lines* are there, waiting to take you in."[8]

Notes

Introduction

1 Everett True, "Massive: Surrender to the Rhythm," *Melody Maker* (April 13, 1991), 44.

2 Quoted in Sean O'Hagan, "Blue Lines: Massive Attack's Blueprint for UK's Pop Future," *Guardian* (October 27, 2012). Online at: https://www.theguardian.com/music/2012/oct/28/massive-attack-blue-lines-remaster. Accessed September 2018.

Chapter 1

1 Del Naja, quoted in John Robb, "Shipshape & Bristol Fashion," *The Quietus* (February 10, 2010). Online at: http://thequietus.com/articles/03708-massive-attack-interview-heligoland-john-robb. Accessed August 2018.

2 Nolan, quoted in "Sex Pistols Gig: The Truth," *BBC* (September 24, 2014). Online at: http://www.bbc.co.uk/manchester/content/articles/2006/05/11/110506_sex_pistols_gig_feature.shtml. Accessed August 2018. See also Nolan's book, *I Swear I Was There: The Gig That Changed the World* (London: Music Press Books, 2006).

3 All Rob Smith quotes from interview with the author, October 2017. Audio recording and author's transcript.

4 Del Naja, quoted in Robb, "Shipshape & Bristol Fashion."

5 Hill has some rather humorous recollections of the short-lived group, including the observation that Hooper, later of Wild Bunch and Soul II Soul fame, is someone whose "career is well documented and for someone with limited talent he appears to have done rather well!" See "Mouth," *Bristol Archive Records.* Online at: http://bristolarchiverecords.com/bands/Mouth.html. Accessed August 2018.

6 Cherry, quoted in Richard Gehr, "Neneh Cherry Talks Her Weird Punk-Pop-Jazz Trajectory, and the New 'Blank Project,'" *Spin* (February 24, 2014). Online at: https://www.spin.com/2014/02/neneh-cherry-interview-blank-project/.

7 Isaac Hayes also did a version of "The Look of Love" in 1970. While his ultra-smooth rendition is updated for a hip-hop generation, he is cited as an influence in the liner notes to *Blue Lines.*

8 See Peter Webb, *Exploring the Networked Worlds of Popular Music* (London: Routledge, 2007), 59.

Chapter 2

1 Quoted in "Interview with Massive Attack," *Q Radio* (Winter 2010), author's audio recording.

2 Grandmaster Flash and the Furious Five's "The Message" (1982) is an obvious exception, and an augur of things to come.

3 See Campbell's own account in Jeff Chang, *Can't Stop Won't Stop: A History of the Hip-Hop Generation* (New York: Picador, 2005).

4   For more on the history of reggae and dub in the United
    Kingdom, see Julian Henriques, *Sonic Bodies: Reggae Sound
    Systems, Performance Techniques, and Ways of Knowing*
    (London: Continuum, 2011). Of course, the deep grooves,
    syncopated rhythms, and blazing horns of American funk
    found its parallel globally as well, as in then-contemporary
    Nigerian afrobeat and Ghanaian highlife music.

5   Though a great deal of oral history abounds online. See, for
    instance, Andy Bassford, "The Coxsone I Knew: Memories of
    Studio One in Brooklyn" (2013). Online at: andybassford.com.
    Accessed August 2018. Journalistic accounts of visits to reggae
    producers (especially during the popular heyday of the 1970s)
    are also illuminating. A more recent example is John Jeremiah
    Sullivan's "The Last Wailer," *Pulphead* (New York: Farrar, Straus
    & Giroux, 2011), 279–307.

6   Ray Mighty, interview with author, October 13, 2017.

7   Quoted in interview with the author, December 12, 2016. Also
    see his *Roots & Culture: Cultural Politics in the Making of Black
    Britain* (London: I.B. Tauris, 2017).

Chapter 3

1   Their jam "Keep on Movin,'" with its lush orchestral moves and
    video featuring Hindu iconography similarly looked ahead
    to Massive's "Unfinished Sympathy" and "Hymn of the Big
    Wheel."

2   Quoted in "Interview with Massive Attack," *Q Radio*.

3   "Interview with Massive Attack," *KCRW Radio* (Winter 2010),
    author's audiorecording.

4   Allan also worked on a project called a "transputer," a parallel array processor setup that now has applications in everything from music to graphics to AI.

5   People are surprised to hear that Hackwell has the space up and running. The Coach House has long been considered abandoned. Its heyday was roughly a decade, ending, along with many other things in the industry, around 1999, but during this time, the space was inaugurated by an all-woman ska band called Meet Your Feet and any number of local acts looking to cut a three-track demo. Allan was a boon to such groups, many of whom could play instruments, but needed someone not only to let the studio but to act as engineer and producer, gaming out how to achieve a sound using the complex tools at hand. Allan usually started by making groups break down the songs into the once-standard eight tracks of the recording machine of the same name. From there, songs could be built, bit by bit, gaming out phrases and layers with an eye toward not losing fidelity as things got bounced across channels, and from tape to tape.

6   All Andy Allan quotations from interview with the author, October 2017, audio recording and author's transcript.

Chapter 4

1   If you care to rehash the critical reductionism of the time, there's plenty of it. There are also titles on the individual groups, including 33 1/3 no. 85, on the 1994 Portishead classic *Dummy*. See, for example, Phil Johnson, *Straight Outta Bristol: Massive Attack, Portishead, Tricky, and the Roots of Trip-Hop* (London: Coronet, 1997).

2 Dele Fadele, "The Severn Alliance," *New Musical Express* (February 18, 1995), 48.

3 Gonzalez, correspondence with the author, June 30, 2018.

4 Tricky, "In Conversation—Knowle West Boy," *Domino Records Promotional Video* (2008). Online at: https://www.youtube.com/watch?v=TGI2UGKb72w.

5 See Dave Simpson, "30 Minutes with Tricky," *Guardian* (May 23, 2013). Online at: https://www.theguardian.com/music/2013/may/23/tricky-i-dont-believe-death-exists#2. Accessed January 2019.

6 Quoted in Euromag, "Tricky Breaks 5-yr Silence with Vibrant 'Knowle West Boy,'" *Euronews* (November 9, 2008). Online at: https://www.euronews.com/2008/09/11/tricky-breaks-5-yr-studio-silence-with-vibrant-knowle-west-boy. Accessed February 2019.

7 Tellingly, this piece wasn't even written by an American journalist, but was submitted by Ekow Eshun, the Ghanaian—British curator of contemporary art, whose brother, Kodwo, is a theorist of science fiction and diasporic music. See Ekow Eshun, "Tricky: Britain's Bad Boy of Trip Hop," *Vibe* (September, 1995), 68. Also, Kodwo Eshun, *More Brilliant Than the Sun: Adventures in Sonice Fiction* (New York: Interlink, 1999).

8 In David Bowie, "You Don't Wanna Be Painting Your Face Like That," *Q Magazine* (October 1995), no page numbers.

9 There are some clear historical precedents and thoughtful academic ways of describing what Tricky is up to here. Historian Tobias Wofford, for instance, looks back to South Chicago and a branch of the American Black Arts Movement known as AfriCOBRA. The collective worked in opposition to the mainstream (white) art world of the 1960s and 1970s and looked to create pan-African connections. Britain had its own

corollaries of the Black Panthers and the Black Arts Movement at roughly this time, reaching a crescendo of influence by the late 1980s, when theorists like Paul Gilroy were postulating the existence of a Black Atlantic world that underpinned and operated beyond the confines of our traditional maps of knowledge and power. Within such a diasporic world, Africa and the Caribbean, Brixton and Brooklyn are all connected by memory, fantasy, shared history and exchanged culture—especially music. Wofford talks about a specific kind of diasporic temporality, one marked by "anamnesis," a simultaneous looking to the future and the past, to one's roots and to a visionary path yet to unfold. In this account, America is no longer at the center it so often occupies in culture, and daily life in Britain, too, would take on the counters of, in Rastafarian terms, a fallen Babylon, a corrupted material plane. See Tobias Wofford, "Afrofutures," *Third Text* 31 (2017): 633–49. doi: https://doi.org/10.1080/09528822.2018.1431472

10 It should be noted here that the sections above, describing Tricky as a Bowie figure and an aerial are both verbatim echoed in the Reynolds piece, although they were written without my having yet carefully read his account. Maybe I absorbed his influence through the ether; maybe these are just the evident ways to describe Tricky. But, credit where credit is due: thank you Simon. For these descriptions, and the quotations below, see his *Energy Flash: A Journey Through Rave Music and Dance Culture* (New York: Soft Skull, 1998), 314–34.

Interlude

1 These quotations are from Simon Reynolds, *Energy Flash: A Journey Through Rave Music and Dance Culture* (Berkeley: Soft Skull Press, 1998), 314. The title of this chapter, it should be

noted, is a subheading in Reynolds's own, which doesn't make it any less apt.

2 More to the point, Smith's subsequent films, such as *Chasing Amy* located the epicenter of such banter, appropriately, at the redoubts of bored suburbanites—mostly men—at the comic emporium, a place where frivolous distinctions and valuations within pulp genres could be spoken of with the erudition of a cleric, archives, and provenance maintained with curatorial zeal, neophytes cast aside with snide derision.

3 See Todd Boyd, "Check Yo Self before You Wreck Yo Self: The Death of Politics in Rap Music and Popular Culture," in *That's the Joint! The Hip-Hop Studies Reader*, eds. Murray Forman and Mark Anthony Neal (New York: Routledge, 2004), 325–40.

4 Championship Vinyl is both a kind of brick-andmortar echo of another Chicago outfit—Pitchfork Media (also founded 1995)—and an index fossil for the way "serious people" (read: neurotic white people) thought about underground music in the 1990s.

5 LCD Soundsystem's own "Losing My Edge" mocks and mourns the coming of the internet and the passage of time, which rendered the knowledge won of record stores (so central to 1990s-era cultural distinction) obsolete. Incidentally, Murphy also wrote one called "You Wanted a Hit" that calls out the record store snobs and Pitchfork Medias of the world "No, honestly, you know too much/So leave us, leave us on our own." Incidentally, Pitchfork recognizes *Blue Lines* as a record of epochal importance (9 forks out of 10!). See Myles Raymer, "Massive Attack: Blue Lines," *Pitchfork* (September 30, 2012). Online: https://pitchfork.com/reviews/albums/17384-blue-lines-remastered-box-set/.

6 Reynolds, *Energy Flash*, 315.

7   On this, see David Samuels, "The Rap on Rap," *The New Republic* (November 11, 1991), 20–24.

8   Ultrasonic, in turn, is known for upbeat tracks in the post-Acid mold, dreamy house records with samples of Nina Simone (e.g., Radiant Baby's "New Dawn") suited to the United Kingdom's embryonic rave culture.

9   Jack Garofalo, "Massive Attack's 'Ritual Spirit,'" *The Source* (March 3, 2016). Online at: http://thesource.com/2016/03/03/britisheuropean-album-of-the-month-massive-attacks-ritual-spirit/. The reviewer further points to sometimes Massive collaborator Roots Manuva as "the godfather" of British hip-hop. It should be noted that the latter's debut was 1994—albeit an excellent moment for art and music in the United Kingdom—but also several years after the release of *Blue Lines* and partway into hip-hop's third decade back in the United States.

10 There is some debate on this, but the "golden age" of hip-hop general spans the second half of the 1980s, roughly 1987 to 1992.

11 Raymer, "Massive Attack: Blue Lines."

12 Simon Reynolds, "Psychedelic Rock Enters the Progressive Phase," *New York Times* (April 18, 1991), 23.

Chapter 5

1   These last two examples, it should be noted, are remarkable videos in their own right, nearly lost to the sands of time. If you'd like to understand 1991 in pure, crystalline form, please take a moment to refer to YouTube.

2   Deidre Dyer, "The Unsung '80s Style Movement That Predicted Fashion's Genderless Present: Interview with Barry Kamen and Jamie Morgan," *The Fader* (August 25, 2015), online.

3 Quoted in Jamie Morgan, "The Spirit of Buffalo." Online at: http://www.thefader.com/2015/08/25/spirit-of-buffalo-interview-dr-martens. Accessed June 21, 2018. See also Buffalo, Westzone Publishing, London, 2000_Smile i-D, Taschen, 2000.

4 See Tim Lawrence, *Love Saves the Day: A History of American Dance Music Culture, 1970-1970* (Durham, NC and London: Duke University Press, 2003). Also, Peter Hook, *The Hacienda: How Not to Run a Club* (London: Simon & Schuster UK, 2009). And Michaelangelo Matos, "Shoom: An Oral History of the London Club that Kicked Off Rave Culture," *Rolling Stone* (December 12, 2017). Online at: https://www.rollingstone.com/music/features/shoom-inside-the-dance-club-that-kicked-off-rave-culture-w513097. Accessed June 20, 2017.

5 His classic 1987 record "Beat Dis" is arguably one of the first industrial records. It's the missing link between and Phuture's "Acid Trax" and Nine Inch Nails's Pretty Hate Machine, with a dash of NYC breakbeats and a pinch of Ennio Morricone. It's insane, and the music video favorably pairs Steve McQueen muscle car antics with archival footage of nuclear testing, alongside 1980s-vintage skate and b-boy culture.

6 See "The Rise of Neneh Cherry" (1989), reformatted VHS cassette, available online at: https://vimeo.com/93425488. Accessed June 22, 2017.

Chapter 6

1 Banksy's global notoriety was undoubtedly accelerated by the rapid traffic of images on the internet. But his success is also rooted in the same soil as the career of someone like Damien Hirst, another Bristol artist who, during his time at

Goldsmiths from 1987 to 1989 realized three things: 1. There was loads of money to be made in the art world, not only as a maker but also as a savvy "creative director" of one's own brand; 2. There was loads of money to be made by thumbing one's nose at systems of institutional authority in the name of the avant-garde while also exploiting those systems; and 3. There was loads of money to be made by working at a slight remove from the galleries, curating DIY shows in the disused spaces of global capitalism, like in the London docklands. The latter—staging shows such as 1988's Freeze—was, at the time, seen as just the sort of enterprising fusion of art world glitz and resourceful punk rock brio that might be the stuff of a whole new London art boom. It was, and as a result that fine line between selling out and buying in became finer still. But that's a story for another book.

Suffice it to say, for now, that Damien Hirst revels in art world celebrity—even selling his work at private auction to maximize profits and bypass galleries altogether.

2 Michael Yong, "Banksy Denies He Is Robert Del Naja from Massive Attack in Rare Interview," *BristolLive* (August 3, 2017). Online at: https://www.bristolpost.co.uk/news/bristol-news/banksy-denies-robert-del-naja-278582.

3 Roisin O'Connor, "Who Is Robert Del Naja? The Massive Attack Singer Everyone Believes Is Banksy," *Independent* (June 23, 2017). Online at: https://www.independent.co.uk/arts-entertainment/music/news/robert-del-naja-banksy-who-is-he-goldie-massive-attack-singer-graffiti-artist-bristol-a7805386.html.

4 Quoted in "Interview with Robert Del Naja," *3D and the Art of Massive Attack* (London: The Vinyl Factory, 2015), unpaginated.

5   Both quotations from The Art of 3D and Massive Attack, unpaginated.

6   Ibid.

7   Ibid.

8   Ibid.

9   Ariella Gittlin, "How Feminist Artists Reclaimed Futura from New York's Mad Men," *Artsy* (August 11, 2017), n.p. Online at: https://www.artsy.net/article/artsy-editorial-feminist-artists-reclaimed-futura-new-yorks-mad-men.

Chapter 7

1   Quoted in Michael A. Gonzalez, "Twenty Years Later: On Massive Attack and Mezzanine," *The Paris Review* (April 20, 2018), n.p. Online at: https://www.theparisreview.org/blog/2018/04/20/twenty-years-later-on-massive-attack-and-mezzanine/.

2   See O'Hagan, "Blue Lines."

3   Del Naja's recollections, as well as Nelson and Malone quotes are in "The Making of Unfinished Sympathy by Massive Attack," archival scan, n.p. Online at: https://massiveattack.ie/scans/uncut-magazine-feature/. Accessed September 2018.

4   All Walsh quotes from an interview with the author, March 30, 2018. Author's transcript.

5   Quoted in "Interview with Massive Attack," *The Raft/NME*, author's audiorecording.

Chapter 8

1 The feature is online at: https://www.rollingstone.com/music/music-lists/500-greatest-albums-of-all-time-156826/massive-attack-blue-lines-66986/. Accessed September 2018.

2 Review available online at: https://pitchfork.com/reviews/albums/17384-blue-lines-remastered-box-set/. Accessed September 2018.

3 In "Interview with Massive Attack," *Q Radio*.

4 Quoted in "Interview with Massive Attack," *Q Radio*.

5 This is in Fisher's *Ghosts of my Life: Writing on Depression, Hauntology and Lost Futures* (London: Zero, 2014).

6 In "Interview with Massive Attack," *Q Radio*.

7 For Simon Reynolds, a key development in electronic music was its shift away from roots in soul, disco, house, and other black musics and toward a decidedly computerized and "unfunky" mode. See, for instance, *Retromania: Pop Culture's Addiction to Its Own Past* (New York: Farrar, Straus & Giroux, 2011).

8 Quoted in Everett True, "Massive: Surrender to the Rhythm," *Melody Maker* (April 13, 1991), 45.

Also available in the series

1. *Dusty Springfield's Dusty in Memphis* by Warren Zanes
2. *Love's Forever Changes* by Andrew Hultkrans
3. *Neil Young's Harvest* by Sam Inglis
4. *The Kinks' The Kinks Are the Village Green Preservation Society* by Andy Miller
5. *The Smiths' Meat Is Murder* by Joe Pernice
6. *Pink Floyd's The Piper at the Gates of Dawn* by John Cavanagh
7. *ABBA's ABBA Gold: Greatest Hits* by Elisabeth Vincentelli
8. *The Jimi Hendrix Experience's Electric Ladyland* by John Perry
9. *Joy Division's Unknown Pleasures* by Chris Ott
10. *Prince's Sign "☮" the Times* by Michaelangelo Matos
11. *The Velvet Underground's The Velvet Underground & Nico* by Joe Harvard
12. *The Beatles' Let It Be* by Steve Matteo
13. *James Brown's Live at the Apollo* by Douglas Wolk
14. *Jethro Tull's Aqualung* by Allan Moore
15. *Radiohead's OK Computer* by Dai Griffiths
16. *The Replacements' Let It Be* by Colin Meloy
17. *Led Zeppelin's Led Zeppelin IV* by Erik Davis
18. *The Rolling Stones' Exile on Main St.* by Bill Janovitz
19. *The Beach Boys' Pet Sounds* by Jim Fusilli
20. *Ramones' Ramones* by Nicholas Rombes
21. *Elvis Costello's Armed Forces* by Franklin Bruno
22. *R.E.M.'s Murmur* by J. Niimi
23. *Jeff Buckley's Grace* by Daphne Brooks
24. *DJ Shadow's Endtroducing…..* by Eliot Wilder

25. *MC5's Kick Out the Jams* by Don McLeese

26. *David Bowie's Low* by Hugo Wilcken

27. *Bruce Springsteen's Born in the U.S.A.* by Geoffrey Himes

28. *The Band's Music from Big Pink* by John Niven

29. *Neutral Milk Hotel's In the Aeroplane over the Sea* by Kim Cooper

30. *Beastie Boys' Paul's Boutique* by Dan Le Roy

31. *Pixies' Doolittle* by Ben Sisario

32. *Sly and the Family Stone's There's a Riot Goin' On* by Miles Marshall Lewis

33. *The Stone Roses' The Stone Roses* by Alex Green

34. *Nirvana's In Utero* by Gillian G. Gaar

35. *Bob Dylan's Highway 61 Revisited* by Mark Polizzotti

36. *My Bloody Valentine's Loveless* by Mike McGonigal

37. *The Who's The Who Sell Out* by John Dougan

38. *Guided by Voices' Bee Thousand* by Marc Woodworth

39. *Sonic Youth's Daydream Nation* by Matthew Stearns

40. *Joni Mitchell's Court and Spark* by Sean Nelson

41. *Guns N' Roses' Use Your Illusion I and II* by Eric Weisbard

42. *Stevie Wonder's Songs in the Key of Life* by Zeth Lundy

43. *The Byrds' The Notorious Byrd Brothers* by Ric Menck

44. *Captain Beefheart's Trout Mask Replica* by Kevin Courrier

45. *Minutemen's Double Nickels on the Dime* by Michael T. Fournier

46. *Steely Dan's Aja* by Don Breithaupt

47. *A Tribe Called Quest's People's Instinctive Travels and the Paths of Rhythm* by Shawn Taylor

48. *PJ Harvey's Rid of Me* by Kate Schatz

49. *U2's Achtung Baby* by Stephen Catanzarite

50. *Belle & Sebastian's If You're Feeling Sinister* by Scott Plagenhoef

51. *Nick Drake's Pink Moon* by Amanda Petrusich

52. *Celine Dion's Let's Talk About Love* by Carl Wilson

53. *Tom Waits' Swordfishtrombones* by David Smay

54. *Throbbing Gristle's 20 Jazz Funk Greats* by Drew Daniel

55. *Patti Smith's Horses* by Philip Shaw

56. *Black Sabbath's Master of Reality* by John Darnielle

57. *Slayer's Reign in Blood* by D.X. Ferris

58. *Richard and Linda Thompson's Shoot Out the Lights* by Hayden Childs

59. *The Afghan Whigs' Gentlemen* by Bob Gendron

60. *The Pogues' Rum, Sodomy, and the Lash* by Jeffery T. Roesgen

61. *The Flying Burrito Brothers' The Gilded Palace of Sin* by Bob Proehl

62. *Wire's Pink Flag* by Wilson Neate

63. *Elliott Smith's XO* by Mathew Lemay

64. *Nas' Illmatic* by Matthew Gasteier

65. *Big Star's Radio City* by Bruce Eaton

66. *Madness' One Step Beyond…* by Terry Edwards

67. *Brian Eno's Another Green World* by Geeta Dayal

68. *The Flaming Lips' Zaireeka* by Mark Richardson

69. *The Magnetic Fields' 69 Love Songs* by LD Beghtol

70. *Israel Kamakawiwo'ole's Facing Future* by Dan Kois

71. *Public Enemy's It Takes a Nation of Millions to Hold Us Back* by Christopher R. Weingarten

72. *Pavement's Wowee Zowee* by Bryan Charles

73. *AC/DC's Highway to Hell* by Joe Bonomo

74. *Van Dyke Parks's Song Cycle* by Richard Henderson

75. *Slint's Spiderland* by Scott Tennent

76. *Radiohead's Kid A* by Marvin Lin

77. *Fleetwood Mac's Tusk* by Rob Trucks

78. *Nine Inch Nails' Pretty Hate Machine* by Daphne Carr

79. *Ween's Chocolate and Cheese* by Hank Shteamer

80. *Johnny Cash's American Recordings* by Tony Tost

81. *The Rolling Stones' Some Girls* by Cyrus Patell

82. *Dinosaur Jr.'s You're Living All Over Me* by Nick Attfield

83. *Television's Marquee Moon* by Bryan Waterman

84. *Aretha Franklin's Amazing Grace* by Aaron Cohen

85. *Portishead's Dummy* by RJ Wheaton

86. *Talking Heads' Fear of Music* by Jonathan Lethem

87. *Serge Gainsbourg's Histoire de Melody Nelson* by Darran Anderson

88. *They Might Be Giants' Flood* by S. Alexander Reed and Philip Sandifer

89. *Andrew W.K.'s I Get Wet* by Phillip Crandall

90. *Aphex Twin's Selected Ambient Works Volume II* by Marc Weidenbaum

91. *Gang of Four's Entertainment* by Kevin J.H. Dettmar

92. *Richard Hell and the Voidoids' Blank Generation* by Pete Astor

93. *J Dilla's Donuts* by Jordan Ferguson

94. *The Beach Boys' Smile* by Luis Sanchez

95. *Oasis' Definitely Maybe* by Alex Niven

96. *Liz Phair's Exile in Guyville* by Gina Arnold

97. *Kanye West's My Beautiful Dark Twisted Fantasy* by Kirk Walker Graves

98. *Danger Mouse's The Grey Album* by Charles Fairchild

99. *Sigur Rós's ()* by Ethan Hayden

100. *Michael Jackson's Dangerous* by Susan Fast

101. *Can's Tago Mago* by Alan Warner

102. *Bobbie Gentry's Ode to Billie Joe* by Tara Murtha

103. *Hole's Live Through This* by Anwen Crawford

104. *Devo's Freedom of Choice* by Evie Nagy

105. *Dead Kennedys' Fresh Fruit for Rotting Vegetables* by Michael Stewart Foley

106. *Koji Kondo's Super Mario Bros.* by Andrew Schartmann

107. *Beat Happening's Beat Happening* by Bryan C. Parker

108. *Metallica's Metallica* by David Masciotra

109. *Phish's A Live One* by Walter Holland

110. *Miles Davis' Bitches Brew* by George Grella Jr.

111. *Blondie's Parallel Lines* by Kembrew McLeod

112. *Grateful Dead's Workingman's Dead* by Buzz Poole

113. *New Kids On The Block's Hangin' Tough* by Rebecca Wallwork

114. *The Geto Boys' The Geto Boys* by Rolf Potts

115. *Sleater-Kinney's Dig Me Out* by Jovana Babovic

116. *LCD Soundsystem's Sound of Silver* by Ryan Leas

117. *Donny Hathaway's Donny Hathaway Live* by Emily J. Lordi

118. *The Jesus and Mary Chain's Psychocandy* by Paula Mejia

119. *The Modern Lovers' The Modern Lovers* by Sean L. Maloney

120. *Angelo Badalamenti's Soundtrack from Twin Peaks* by Clare Nina Norelli

121. *Young Marble Giants' Colossal Youth* by Michael Blair and Joe Bucciero

122. *The Pharcyde's Bizarre Ride II the Pharcyde* by Andrew Barker

123. *Arcade Fire's The Suburbs* by Eric Eidelstein

124. *Bob Mould's Workbook* by Walter Biggins and Daniel Couch

125. *Camp Lo's Uptown Saturday Night* by Patrick Rivers and Will Fulton

126. *The Raincoats' The Raincoats* by Jenn Pelly

127. *Björk's Homogenic* by Emily Mackay

128. *Merle Haggard's Okie from Muskogee* by Rachel Lee Rubin

129. *Fugazi's In on the Kill Taker* by Joe Gross

130. *Jawbreaker's 24 Hour Revenge Therapy* by Ronen Givony

131. *Lou Reed's Transformer* by Ezra Furman

132. *Drive-By Truckers' Southern Rock Opera* by Rien Fertel

133. *Siouxsie and the Banshees' Peepshow* by Samantha Bennett

134. *dc Talk's Jesus Freak* by Will Stockton and D. Gilson

135. *Tori Amos's Boys for Pele* by Amy Gentry

136. *Odetta's One Grain of Sand* by Matthew Frye Jacobson

137. *Manic Street Preachers' The Holy Bible* by David Evans

138. *The Shangri-Las' Golden Hits of the Shangri-Las* by Ada Wolin

139. *Tom Petty's Southern Accents* by Michael Washburn